The Desert Between Us

Not all love is meant to be lived.

Christine Zanjanipour

ISBN: 979-8-9939013-8-1

First Edition

Published by Details Matter Books

Printed in the United States of America

www.DetailsMatterBooks.com

For Gordy and Karen

thank you for a journey that never truly ended.

There are people who feel like memories,
even the first time you meet them.

CHAPTER ONE

The City of Fire

The plane descended through a haze that did not look like cloud.

Elara Quinn leaned toward the window, her forehead resting lightly against the glass as she searched the darkness below for something familiar, something grounding. Instead, the city revealed itself slowly, its lights diffused through a veil of smoke that softened every edge. Gold blurred into amber. White lights pulsed faintly through the thickened air. It felt less like landing and more like entering something already in motion.

She had not slept.

Fourteen hours in the air had passed in fragments of awareness. A few moments with her eyes closed. A brief drift into something that almost resembled rest before her thoughts pulled her back again. Around her, the cabin had surrendered hours ago. Passengers folded into themselves beneath thin blankets. Heads tilted at awkward angles. The quiet murmur of breathing layered over the steady hum of the engines.

But Elara remained awake.

She had spent most of the flight staring at nothing, or at everything. The condensation sliding slowly down the side of her glass. The reflection of her own face in the darkened window, distorted by the curve of the glass and the faint glow of the cabin lights. She had tried to read. Tried to review notes for the assignment. Tried to convince herself that this trip was about work.

It was, in part.

But not entirely.

Luca had a way of staying with her.

Not loudly. Not in any way that demanded attention. He lingered in quieter ways. In the spaces between thoughts. In the moments when she should have been focused on something else.

She closed her eyes, but the memory came anyway.

The last night had not been dramatic.

There had been no raised voices. No final words worth remembering. That almost made it worse.

He had been standing near the window of her apartment, buttoning his shirt with the same unhurried ease he brought to everything. As if time bent around him. As if nothing required explanation.

She had said his name once.

Just once.

He had looked at her then, briefly, something soft flickering across his expression before it disappeared.

"I'll call you," he had said.

He always said that.

She had known, even then, that he wouldn't.

Still, she had nodded.

As if agreement could soften the truth.

As if pretending not to know would make it hurt less.

It never did.

The plane touched down with a quiet jolt that pulled her back into the present.

A subtle shift in gravity. The engines lowering. The collective exhale of a cabin returning to ground.

India.

She had been here before.

But this felt different.

By the time she stepped out of the airport, the night had already wrapped itself around her.

Heat pressed gently against her skin, thick but not suffocating. It carried with it a complexity of scent that arrived all at once and then slowly separated into something she could begin to understand.

Smoke.

Spice.

Dust.

Something sweet.

She paused at the curb, her suitcase at her side, letting it settle.

Above her, the sky split open in gold.

A firework climbed, burst, and scattered light across the haze. Another followed, then another, each one echoing through the night with a sharp, hollow crack that lingered longer than it should have.

Diwali.

The festival of lights.

She had not planned for this.

Or maybe she had not allowed herself to think that far ahead.

The street in front of the airport moved with a kind of restless energy that felt both chaotic and precise.

Cars pressed forward in uneven lines, horns sounding in short bursts that layered into something strangely rhythmic. Motorbikes slipped between them with impossible ease. Families moved together along the edges of the road, their clothing catching the light in flashes of color. Deep reds. Burnt oranges. Gold thread that shimmered with every movement.

Children ran ahead of their parents, sparklers in their hands, leaving trails of light that vanished almost as quickly as they appeared.

The air shifted again as a breeze moved through.

This time, she caught something new.

Cardamom.

Warm, almost floral.

Then something deeper.

Cumin.

Toasted. Earthy.

And beneath it, the unmistakable richness of something frying in oil. Street food she could not see but could almost taste. Savory. Spiced. Layered with heat and sweetness at once.

Her senses struggled to keep up.

Everything demanded attention.

Everything felt amplified.

"Miss Quinn."

She turned at the sound of her name.

A man stood a few feet away, holding a small placard with her name printed in careful black letters. His expression was composed, his posture relaxed, his presence grounding in a way she had not expected.

She nodded and moved toward him.

The drive into the city unfolded like a series of moving images she could not fully absorb.

Fireworks continued overhead, their reflections flickering across the windshield. Roads narrowed and widened without warning. Buildings rose and disappeared into the haze. At one intersection, a group of men stood around a small fire, feeding it with scraps of wood and paper. The flames cast shifting shadows across their faces.

At another, a woman sat near the edge of the road, arranging small clay lamps in precise rows, each one glowing softly, their light steady and deliberate.

Elara rolled the window down slightly.

The air rushed in, warmer now, thicker with scent.

Jasmine.

Faint, but unmistakable.

It wove through everything else, softening the smoke, lifting the spice, creating something unexpectedly delicate in the midst of it all.

She closed her eyes for a moment, letting it settle.

New York felt far away.

Not in distance.

In feeling.

There, everything had been sharp. Defined. Fast.

Here, everything blurred at the edges, as if the world itself was less concerned with precision and more interested in experience.

She found herself breathing differently.

Slower.

Deeper.

Her hotel appeared almost suddenly, set back from the road behind a low wall and iron gates.

The shift was immediate.

Noise softened.

Movement slowed.

The chaos of the street seemed to pause just outside, as if held back by something unseen.

Inside, the air was cooler.

Quieter.

The scent changed again. Less smoke. Less spice. Something cleaner, but still touched by the outside world in a way that felt intentional.

She checked in, her voice sounding distant even to her own ears.

Her body was beginning to register the exhaustion she had been holding at bay.

In her room, she set her bag down near the bed and stood still.

For a long moment, she did nothing.

Just listened.

To the muted echo of fireworks outside. To the faint hum of the building. To her own breathing.

This was supposed to be simple.

An assignment.

A story.

A place she would visit, document, and leave.

But standing there, in the quiet after everything she had just moved through, she felt something else begin to surface.

Not excitement.

Not anticipation.

Something quieter.

More certain.

She moved to the window and pulled the curtain aside.

The city stretched out before her, still alive, still burning with light.

And for the first time since leaving New York, she noticed something.

She was not thinking about Luca.

Not in the way she had been.

The sharpness had softened.

The urgency had faded.

It was still there.

But it was no longer the center of everything.

She let the curtain fall.

Tomorrow, she would leave the city.

A long drive west.

Into the desert.

Into something she did not yet understand.

Elara sat at the edge of the bed, her hands resting loosely in her lap.

There was space inside her now.

Not empty.

Just open.

As if something had shifted.

Quietly.

Without asking her permission.

She lay back, the sounds of the city continuing just beyond the walls.

Another firework split the sky outside.

Light flickered briefly against the ceiling before fading again.

She closed her eyes.

She had told herself this trip was about work.

About photographs.

About capturing something rare and fleeting.

But somewhere beneath that, a quieter truth had already begun to take shape.

She had not come here just to see something new.

She had come here to become someone she had not yet been able to be.

And she did not yet realize it.

But the woman she had been in New York was already beginning to disappear.

CHAPTER TWO

The Road West

Morning came softly.

Elara woke before the alarm, her body unsure of time, her mind already alert in a way that felt unfamiliar after the long flight. For a moment, she lay still, listening.

The city had changed.

The sharp bursts of fireworks were gone, replaced by something steadier. A distant hum. Movement without urgency. Voices layered beneath the sound of traffic. Somewhere below, metal clinked against metal. A cart being pushed. A gate opening. Life beginning again.

She sat up slowly, the weight of travel still lingering in her limbs, and crossed the room to the window.

The haze had lifted just enough to reveal the outlines of buildings stretching into the distance. The light was pale, almost diffused, softening the edges of everything it touched. Below, the streets were already alive. Vendors setting up. Motorbikes weaving between cars. Women in bright fabrics moving with quiet purpose.

India did not wait for anyone to wake up.

It simply continued.

By the time she made her way downstairs, her camera bag slung across her shoulder, the hotel lobby was calm, almost removed from the world outside. A faint scent of tea lingered in the air, something warm and spiced.

Cardamom again.

She paused briefly, taking it in.

Her driver was waiting.

He stood just outside the entrance, leaning lightly against the car, his posture relaxed but attentive. When he saw her, he straightened and offered a small nod.

"Good morning, Miss Quinn."

"Good morning," she replied, returning the nod.

He introduced himself again, slower this time, giving her space to hear it properly.

"Ravi."

She repeated it, careful with the pronunciation.

"Ravi."

His smile widened slightly.

The city held them for a while.

Traffic moved in slow, unpredictable waves. Cars edged forward, then paused, then moved again. Motorbikes slipped through narrow gaps, their riders balancing with an ease that felt instinctive.

Elara watched everything.

A man carrying a stack of metal containers that seemed too tall to be stable. A woman adjusting the edge of her sari as she walked, her movements fluid and practiced. A boy darting between vehicles, selling small packets of something wrapped in paper.

She lifted her camera but hesitated.

It felt too soon.

She was still observing.

Still adjusting.

Eventually, the city loosened its grip.

The buildings thinned. The roads widened. The air shifted again, losing some of its density, becoming drier, lighter.

Elara rolled the window down halfway.

The breeze carried dust now.

And something else.

Earth.

Open land.

"You have been to India before?" Ravi asked.

"Yes," she said. "But not like this."

He nodded, as if that made sense.

"This is better," he said simply.

She found herself smiling.

The road stretched ahead in a long, unbroken line.

On either side, the landscape unfolded in quiet variation. Small villages appeared and disappeared. Clusters of buildings gathered around narrow roads. Fields extended outward, some green, some dry, each one marked by the slow, deliberate movement of people working within them.

And occasionally, there were camels.

At first, just one or two.

Standing near the road. Moving slowly across the fields. Their shapes distinct against the horizon, almost surreal in their presence.

Elara lifted her camera then.

The instinct returned easily.

She framed the moment. Adjusted for light. Waited for movement.

Click.

The sound grounded her.

They stopped once, just outside a small roadside market.

Ravi gestured toward a cluster of stalls.

"Tea?" he asked.

She hesitated only briefly before nodding.

"Yes."

The air here was richer.

Closer.

The scent of spices was stronger, layered into something almost tangible.

Cumin.

Turmeric.

Ginger.

Something frying nearby sent a wave of warmth through the air, oil popping softly, releasing a savory aroma that made her suddenly aware of how little she had eaten.

Ravi handed her a small cup.

"Chai."

She wrapped her hands around it, feeling the heat seep into her fingers.

The first sip surprised her.

Sweet.

Spiced.

Comforting in a way she had not expected.

They stood there for a moment, not speaking.

Just observing.

People moved around them, engaged in their own rhythms, their own conversations. A woman laughed, the sound bright and unrestrained. A man counted coins into his palm. A child watched Elara openly, curious, unguarded.

She held his gaze for a second, then smiled.

He smiled back.

Back in the car, the landscape began to change again.

Flatter now.

Drier.

The colors shifting toward muted browns and soft golds.

The desert.

She felt it before she fully saw it.

A quiet vastness that seemed to stretch beyond anything she could frame.

Elara leaned her head lightly against the window, her camera resting in her lap.

For the first time in weeks, her mind felt still.

Not empty.

Just… quiet.

She thought about Luca then.

Not sharply.

Not with the same pull.

Just as a memory.

It surprised her.

"You are thinking," Ravi said, glancing at her briefly.

"Yes," she said.

"Good," he replied.

She smiled again, this time without thinking.

Hours passed.

The road continued.

And somewhere along the way, without marking the exact moment, Elara realized something.

She was no longer looking back.

Ahead, the horizon shimmered slightly in the heat.

And beyond it, though she could not yet see it, was something waiting.

She did not know what it was.

But she felt it.

And she was ready.

CHAPTER THREE

The Camp in the Desert

They arrived just before the light began to soften.

The desert stretched wide and uninterrupted, the air carrying a dry warmth that settled differently against her skin. It lacked the density of the city, the layered scents and sounds replaced by something quieter, more expansive.

And then, almost unexpectedly, the camp appeared.

At first, it was only a suggestion.

Shapes against the horizon.

Color against the muted tones of sand.

Then, as they drew closer, it came into focus.

Rows of canvas tents, arranged with a precision that felt intentional but not rigid. Rich fabrics framed each entrance, their colors deep and warm against the pale landscape. And beneath it all, carpets.

Actual carpets.

Laid across the sand in long, continuous paths of red and gold, their patterns intricate, almost too detailed for something temporary.

Elara stepped out of the car slowly.

For a moment, she simply stood there.

Taking it in.

It did not feel like a camp.

It felt like something constructed between worlds.

A young man approached, greeting Ravi first, then turning his attention to her. He took her bag with a polite nod and gestured toward one of the paths.

"Welcome," he said.

As she walked, she noticed the details.

The way the carpets softened the uneven ground. The way the fabric at each tent entrance moved gently with the breeze. The faint scent of something cooking in the distance, layered with spice and warmth.

Cumin again.

And something sweeter.

Perhaps saffron.

Her tent was larger than she expected.

Inside, the light filtered through the canvas in a soft, golden glow. A bed sat in the center, layered with textiles that looked handwoven, slightly imperfect in a way that made them feel more valuable.

There was a small wooden table. A basin. A chair with a folded cloth draped neatly across it.

Simple.

But complete.

"Hot water will come in the morning," the young man said. "For bathing."

She nodded.

The detail stayed with her.

When he left, she moved toward the entrance and stepped back outside.

The air had shifted again.

The light lower now, stretching shadows across the sand.

And in the distance, beyond the final row of tents, there was movement.

Camels.

More than she had ever seen.

Their silhouettes rising and shifting against the horizon, their presence both grounded and surreal.

Men moved among them, their voices carried faintly on the air.

Elara felt something stir inside her.

Not curiosity.

Something stronger.

She adjusted the strap of her camera.

This was why she had come.

Not the city.

Not the assignment.

This.

She stepped forward, just slightly, as if moving closer might bring it into clearer focus.

The sounds drifted toward her.

Low voices.

Movement.

The distant call of animals.

And beneath it all, something she could not yet name.

The beginning of a story.

One she had not yet realized she was already part of.

CHAPTER FOUR

The First Walk into the Fair

The fair did not reveal itself all at once.

It gathered slowly.

At first, it was sound.

Low voices carried over the sand. Men speaking in quick bursts, then pausing. Laughter rising unexpectedly and fading just as fast. The rough, throaty calls of camels moving through the air like something ancient.

Then came movement.

Shapes beyond the camp. Men walking with ropes in their hands. Children weaving through the paths. Animals shifting, lowering, rising, their long legs folding and unfolding with strange grace.

Elara stood at the edge of the carpeted path, camera resting against her hip, and felt the world beyond the camp pulling at her.

Inside the camp, everything was ordered.

Red carpets. Canvas tents. Polished brass pitchers. Staff moving quietly with trays of tea and bowls of food fragrant with cumin, turmeric, coriander, and something sweet she could not name. It was beautiful. Almost unreal.

But outside the camp, beyond the last line of fabric and rugs, the desert was awake.

That was where the story was.

She knew it before she took her first step.

Ravi appeared beside her as if he had known she would not wait long.

"You want to see?" he asked.

She turned to him and smiled.

"Yes."

He nodded once, then gestured toward a wooden cart waiting near the edge of camp.

"We go slowly first."

The cart was simple, its wood worn smooth by use. Two thin cushions had been laid across the seat, but it was still rough beneath her. Elara climbed up, careful with her camera bag, and settled herself as Ravi spoke briefly to the man holding the reins.

A moment later, the cart lurched forward.

The camp slipped behind them.

The fair opened.

Elara had photographed crowded places before. Markets in Morocco. Temples in Thailand. Street festivals in Spain. But this was different. This was not performance. This was not arranged for visitors or softened for outsiders. This world existed with or without her.

And it was enormous.

Camels stretched across the desert in every direction.

Not dozens.

Not hundreds.

Thousands.

They stood in clusters, knelt in rows, moved slowly through the dust with men walking beside them. Their long necks rose above the crowd like watchtowers. Some were plain and muscular, their coats rough, their bodies built for work. Others were decorated with bright cloth and tassels, their faces painted in careful patterns, their bridles adorned with small bells that chimed softly when they moved.

The air was thick with dust and animal heat.

Elara lifted her camera.

The lens found shapes first.

A man in a crimson turban leaning close to examine a camel's teeth.

A boy holding a rope with both hands, his face serious beyond his years.

A group of men sitting in a circle, their palms moving as they negotiated, their expressions impossible to read.

Click.

Click.

Click.

Her breath changed when she worked.

It always did.

The world narrowed and expanded at the same time. Her own life fell away. Her own longing. Her own failures. Behind the camera, she did not have to be the woman who had waited for Luca to call. She did not have to be the friend who smiled through engagement parties and baby showers while wondering what was wrong with her. She did not have to be the daughter explaining, again, why she had chosen another man who could not love her properly.

Behind the camera, she was only seeing.

And here, there was too much to see.

Ravi leaned toward her as the cart moved deeper.

"The fair is not one place," he said. "Many places inside one place."

She lowered the camera slightly.

"What do you mean?"

He pointed toward a wide section to their left.

"Those are working camels. For fields. For carts. Strong ones. Farmers come for them."

Elara turned.

The camels there were broad and steady, their bodies marked by usefulness rather than ornament. Men moved around them with practical focus. They touched legs, shoulders, necks. They watched the animals walk. They discussed endurance, strength, age, price.

There was nothing romantic about it.

No mystery.

Only need.

"These families depend on them," Ravi said. "A good camel changes everything."

Elara nodded, watching a man place a hand against the side of one animal as if feeling for more than muscle. As if he were measuring survival itself.

She raised her camera again.

Click.

The cart continued.

The next section carried a different energy entirely.

Here, the camels were decorated. Their bodies were brushed and painted, draped in fabric, bells, beads, mirrors, and strips of color that caught the light with every movement. Their handlers stood taller. There was pride here, and a kind of theater. Men called out. Buyers circled. Children laughed when one camel turned its head and groaned loudly into the crowd.

Elara smiled despite herself.

This part felt almost celebratory.

Almost safe.

A camel lowered its head near the cart, its large eyes fringed with lashes so long and dark they looked painted. It regarded Elara with a calm, knowing expression.

She laughed softly.

"Beautiful," she said.

Ravi smiled.

"Yes. Beauty has a price also."

They moved on.

The farther they went, the more the fair seemed to change its face.

The noise began to thin.

Not disappear. Never that. But quiet itself became noticeable, tucked between the sounds. Men stood in smaller groups. Conversations grew lower. The camels here looked different too.

Leaner.

Taller.

More contained.

Their bodies seemed built not for pulling or showing, but for distance. For speed. For disappearing.

Elara noticed the shift before Ravi spoke.

"What is this section?"

Ravi's face changed almost imperceptibly.

"Different camels," he said.

"Different how?"

He looked ahead.

"For the desert."

She waited.

He did not continue.

The cart rolled over a shallow rise in the sand, and suddenly she could see the section more clearly.

There were fewer women here.

Fewer children.

The men watched more carefully. Not just the animals. Everything.

Elara felt the weight of their attention before she understood it.

She lowered her camera.

Ravi noticed.

"Better not take many photos here," he said quietly.

Her pulse quickened.

"Why?"

He took a moment before answering.

"Some camels are known for other work."

The phrase hung between them.

Other work.

Elara looked toward the animals again.

One of them stood apart from the rest, its head lifted, nostrils flaring slightly, its body still but alive with restrained force. It did not look like the others. Not tame exactly. Not wild either.

Trained.

That was the word that came to her.

Trained for something she did not understand.

Ravi kept his voice low.

"People say some can run all night."

She turned to him.

"Run where?"

He did not look at her.

"Across desert. Alone."

A faint chill moved through her despite the heat.

"Alone?"

He nodded once.

"There are stories."

"Tell me."

He glanced at her then, and for the first time since morning his expression held warning.

"Stories are not always good for visitors."

Elara should have let it go.

She knew that.

But curiosity had always been one of her weaknesses. Curiosity, and men who looked like trouble before they even opened their mouths.

"What kind of stories?"

Ravi exhaled softly.

"People say these camels carry things. Things no one speaks about in daylight. They know the route. They run at night. No rider. No lantern."

Elara looked back toward the animals.

The section had become quieter, or perhaps she had stopped hearing anything else.

"And then?"

Ravi's eyes stayed ahead.

"Then they vanish."

"Vanish?"

"In the sand."

She thought she had misunderstood.

"What do you mean?"

"They are trained to lie down in desert," he said. "Very low. Covered by sand. At night, if someone is looking, they see nothing."

Elara felt the image rise in her mind.

A camel moving through darkness, carrying forbidden cargo across the desert. No rider. No voice. Only instinct and training. Then the animal lowering itself into the sand until the night swallowed it.

It sounded impossible.

It sounded like myth.

It sounded exactly like the kind of truth no one would ever put in a magazine.

"What are they carrying?" she asked.

Ravi did not answer at first.

Then, very quietly, he said, "Heroin."

The word fell hard.

It did not belong among the bells and spices and painted camels. It did not belong under the pale sky with the fair stretching outward in color and heat and life.

But there it was.

A darkness beneath the spectacle.

Elara looked down at her camera.

For the first time since arriving, it felt heavy.

Ravi leaned closer.

"You understand now?"

She did.

Or at least, she understood enough.

This was not just a fair.

It was a marketplace of visible and invisible things.

Labor.

Beauty.

Survival.

Status.

Danger.

Secrets.

And somewhere within it all, men who knew how to move through darkness without being seen.

The cart slowed.

Not because Ravi had told it to.

Because someone ahead had stepped into the path.

Elara looked up.

He was standing beside a lean camel the color of wet sand.

At first, she noticed only the shape of him.

Tall, still, composed in a way that made the movement around him seem excessive. His dark hair caught the light where it fell loose near his forehead. His skin was warm brown, his jaw clean and severe, his features sharpened by the desert sun. He wore a white shirt beneath a darker vest, simple but precise, the fabric fitted enough to reveal strength without displaying it.

He was beautiful.

Not in the easy way Luca had been beautiful.

Luca's beauty had announced itself. It entered a room first. It expected to be noticed.

This man did not ask to be seen.

He simply was.

And somehow that made it worse.

Elara felt her throat tighten.

He was speaking to another man, one hand resting lightly on the camel's neck. The animal shifted once, then stilled beneath his touch.

Authority without effort.

That was what she saw.

A man who did not need to raise his voice.

A man others listened to because they already knew they should.

Ravi's posture changed beside her.

Not dramatically.

But enough.

"Who is that?" Elara asked.

Ravi did not answer immediately.

The man turned slightly.

Then his eyes found hers.

The world did not stop.

That was the sort of thing people wrote because they had no better way to describe attraction.

The world did not stop.

The fair continued around them. Men spoke. Camels shifted. Dust lifted in small clouds beneath moving feet.

But something in Elara did.

His eyes were dark and steady. Not curious exactly. Not surprised. He looked at her as if her presence had already been accounted for, as if he had noticed her long before she noticed him.

There was no smile.

No invitation.

Only recognition.

Elara knew she should look away.

She did not.

The cloth at her waist moved slightly in the breeze. Dust touched her lips. She could taste salt, heat, and something metallic in the air.

Still, she held his gaze.

Ravi spoke quietly beside her.

"Arjun Rathore."

The name entered her like a note struck low.

Arjun.

The man looked away first, but not as if he had lost interest.

As if the moment had ended because he had decided it had.

The cart moved again.

Elara did not turn back.

Not immediately.

But she felt him behind her.

She felt the section of the fair they had passed through. The lean camels. The lowered voices. The stories of animals running through the desert at night, carrying what no one dared name in daylight.

She felt Ravi watching her too.

"You should be careful here," he said.

Elara looked at him.

"I am careful."

Ravi's mouth tightened in a way that was almost a smile, but not quite.

"No," he said softly. "You are watching."

The cart continued toward the louder parts of the fair, back toward color and noise and men shouting prices across the sand.

But Elara knew something had changed.

The fair no longer felt like a subject.

It felt like a door.

And without meaning to, without permission, without understanding what waited beyond it, she had already begun to open it.

CHAPTER FIVE

The Weight of Being Seen

By the next morning, the fair had changed again.

Or perhaps Elara had.

The light came differently this time. Clearer. Less diffused by dust. The sky stretched wide and pale above the desert, the early sun casting long shadows that moved slowly across the sand as if time itself had slowed to match the rhythm of the place.

She dressed more carefully.

Not consciously at first. It was only as she adjusted the fabric around her waist, as she chose a lighter blouse and wrapped the cloth more securely along her hips, that she realized she was thinking about how she might be seen.

It was subtle.

But it was there.

The air outside carried the lingering coolness of early morning, but warmth was already building beneath it. Somewhere nearby, breakfast was being prepared. The scent drifted through the camp in soft waves.

Toasted bread.

Spiced potatoes.

Coriander.

Something sweet, almost honeyed, layered beneath it.

Elara paused just outside her tent, closing her eyes briefly as she breathed it in.

The smells here did not sit lightly in the air.

They stayed.

They settled.

They became part of everything.

She ate quickly, though she tasted everything.

The chai was stronger this morning, thicker, the spices more pronounced. Cardamom lingered on her tongue. Ginger warmed the back of her throat. The food was simple but deeply satisfying, each bite carrying flavor that felt intentional rather than decorative.

Even this, she thought, was different.

Nothing here felt accidental.

By the time she reached the edge of the camp, the fair was already in motion.

But the morning carried a different energy.

Less performance.

More purpose.

Men moved with intention. Camels were being led, examined, repositioned. Voices were lower, more focused. Deals beginning rather than unfolding.

Elara adjusted the strap of her camera and stepped forward on foot this time.

No cart.

No distance.

The sand shifted beneath her sandals, uneven and warm, pressing into the soles of her feet as she moved. The sounds grew clearer with every step. The low murmur of conversation. The soft clink of metal. The breath of the animals.

She lifted her camera.

Click.

A man tightening a rope around a camel's neck.

Click.

A boy guiding two animals at once, his hands steady, his movements practiced.

Click.

A woman passing through the edge of the crowd, her sari flowing behind her in a sweep of color that caught the light.

Elara followed the movement instinctively.

And that was when she felt it.

The shift.

It was not loud.

Not obvious.

But it was unmistakable.

Eyes.

She lowered the camera slowly.

At first, it was only one or two people looking at her.

Then more.

Not hostile.

Not welcoming.

Simply aware.

She became aware of herself all at once.

The way her skin caught the light differently. The way her hair moved loosely around her shoulders. The space she occupied as she walked.

In New York, she disappeared into the crowd.

Here, she did not.

Elara continued walking, though her steps slowed.

She adjusted the fabric at her waist again, pulling it slightly higher without fully understanding why.

The awareness settled deeper.

She moved past a group of men seated on low stools, their conversation pausing briefly as she passed. One of them nodded. Another watched her a moment longer than the others.

She kept moving.

The scents shifted as she moved deeper into the fair.

Stronger now.

Animal heat.

Dust.

Leather.

Spices carried on the breeze from food stalls that had begun preparing for the day. Fried dough. Roasted nuts. Something sweet and syrupy that clung to the air.

It was overwhelming.

And yet, she did not want to pull away.

She stopped near a cluster of camels, lifting her camera again.

The lens gave her distance.

Control.

She framed a shot of a camel kneeling in the sand, its long legs folding beneath it, the movement both awkward and graceful at once.

Click.

Behind the camera, she could breathe again.

"Madam."

The voice came from her right.

Soft.

Female.

Elara lowered the camera and turned.

An older woman stood beside her, her presence calm, her expression unreadable but not unkind. Her sari was wrapped tightly, the fabric layered in deep earth tones that blended almost seamlessly with the desert around them.

For a moment, neither of them spoke.

The woman's eyes moved briefly over Elara's face, then down.

To her legs.

Elara followed the glance instinctively.

The fabric she had wrapped that morning had shifted as she walked. It sat lower now, exposing more of her legs than she had realized. The skin, pale against the muted tones of the desert, stood out in a way that felt suddenly obvious.

Exposed.

Before Elara could react, the woman moved.

Without hesitation.

Without asking.

She reached out and gently placed a folded cloth across Elara's legs.

The gesture was light.

Careful.

Almost… protective.

Elara froze.

Not from fear.

From the unexpected intimacy of it.

The cloth settled against her skin, soft and slightly warm from the sun. The woman adjusted it briefly, ensuring it covered what had been exposed, then stepped back.

No words.

Elara opened her mouth, unsure what she meant to say.

"Thank you," she managed, her voice quieter than she intended.

The woman nodded once.

Not smiling.

Not judging.

Simply acknowledging.

And then she was gone.

Elara stood there, the cloth still resting across her legs, her hands hovering just above it as if unsure whether to move it or leave it where it was.

The moment lingered.

Longer than it should have.

It was not embarrassment she felt.

Not exactly.

It was something else.

Awareness.

Of difference.

Of boundaries she had not seen.

Of a world that operated on rules that were never spoken, only understood.

She adjusted the cloth carefully, securing it more firmly around her waist this time.

Her movements slowed.

Her posture shifted.

She was no longer just walking through the fair.

She was moving within it.

The sounds returned gradually.

The voices.

The movement.

The constant rhythm of the place.

But everything felt different now.

Sharper.

More deliberate.

Elara lifted her camera again.

But this time, she paused before taking the shot.

She looked longer.

Waited.

Considered.

She was no longer just capturing images.

She was asking permission.

Even if no one answered.

A breeze moved through the fair, lifting the edge of the cloth slightly before it settled again.

Elara pressed it gently back into place.

And without fully realizing it, she changed.

Not completely.

Not all at once.

But enough.

Somewhere beyond the crowd, beyond the sections she had already explored, beyond the visible layers of the fair, she felt it again.

That pull.

Subtle.

Persistent.

The part of the fair Ravi had warned her about.

The part where the camels stood quieter.

Where the men spoke less.

Where stories moved beneath the surface instead of across it.

She did not go there.

Not yet.

But she knew she would.

Because something in her had already begun to lean in that direction.

And this time…

she was aware of it.

CHAPTER SIX

The Pull

She told herself she would stay closer to the camp that afternoon.

It was a reasonable decision.

There was more than enough to photograph without returning to the far edge of the fair. The sections filled with color, movement, families, traders, decorated camels. Stories that could easily fill an entire assignment without ever stepping into the quieter spaces Ravi had warned her about.

Safe stories.

Beautiful stories.

Stories that would be approved, published, admired.

And yet, as Elara stepped beyond the last line of carpets and into the sand, her body did not follow the plan she had made in her head.

Her feet moved with quiet certainty.

Forward.

Outward.

Toward the part of the fair she had not stopped thinking about.

The air was warmer now, the sun higher, pressing down with a steady intensity that settled into her skin. The scents had deepened with the heat. Dust rose more easily beneath movement. Animal and earth mingled into something raw and unfiltered.

She lifted her camera out of habit, capturing moments as she passed through the more crowded sections.

A man laughing, his teeth bright against sun-darkened skin.

A cluster of boys running barefoot through the sand, chasing each other between the camels.

A woman arranging bangles along her arm, the glass catching the light in small flashes of color.

Click.

Click.

Click.

But her focus was thinner now.

Split.

Part of her still working.

Part of her already elsewhere.

She felt it before she saw it.

That shift.

The way the sound thinned slightly.

The way the air seemed to hold something back.

Elara slowed.

The decorated camels fell behind her. The laughter faded. The calls of traders grew less frequent.

Ahead, the fair rearranged itself into something more contained.

More controlled.

She should turn back.

The thought came clearly this time.

Not as a passing hesitation, but as a deliberate suggestion.

She didn't.

Her steps softened as she moved forward, her body instinctively adjusting. She became aware of the way she carried herself, of the fabric wrapped around her waist, of the way her shoulders held tension she had not noticed before.

The cloth the woman had given her earlier remained secured, covering her legs more fully now.

She touched it briefly as she walked.

A small gesture.

A quiet reminder.

The men here noticed her.

Not in the open, curious way of the morning crowd.

This was different.

More measured.

More intentional.

Their glances were shorter, but sharper. Conversations paused for just a fraction of a second before continuing. Movements shifted, not dramatically, but enough to mark her presence.

Elara kept walking.

Not boldly.

Not timidly.

But with a kind of quiet awareness she had not carried the day before.

She reached the edge of the section and stopped.

Not because she was afraid.

Because she understood she had crossed into something else.

The camels stood in smaller clusters here.

Lean.

Still.

Their bodies held a different kind of tension. Not restless, not agitated, but contained. As if they were waiting for something.

Or trained not to react.

She lifted her camera, then lowered it again.

Not here.

Not yet.

"Elara."

The sound of her name stopped her completely.

Not because it was loud.

Because it was unexpected.

No one here should know her name.

She turned slowly.

He stood several feet away, his presence as steady as she remembered.

Arjun Rathore.

In the full light of day, he was even more striking.

The darkness of his hair contrasted sharply against the brightness of the sky. His features were defined, precise, his expression unreadable in a way that did not invite interpretation. His clothing was simple, but carried with it a quiet authority. Nothing excessive. Nothing careless.

Everything intentional.

Elara felt her pulse shift.

Not racing.

Not panicked.

But present.

"You should not be here alone," he said.

His voice was lower than she expected.

Even.

Controlled.

It was not a question.

"I could say the same to you," she replied.

The words came before she had time to soften them.

A flicker crossed his expression.

Not quite amusement.

Not quite surprise.

Something in between.

"This is my place," he said.

The answer was simple.

Undeniable.

Elara nodded once, acknowledging it.

"And yet," she said, her voice quieter now, "you noticed me."

For a moment, neither of them moved.

The space between them held something that was not entirely comfortable, but not threatening either.

Something charged.

"I noticed you yesterday," he said.

There was no hesitation in it.

No attempt to soften the truth.

Elara felt that.

More than she expected.

"Why?" she asked.

He took a step closer.

Not enough to close the distance completely.

Just enough to shift it.

"You look at things differently," he said.

She frowned slightly.

"That's my job."

He shook his head, almost imperceptibly.

"No," he said. "That is not what I mean."

Silence settled between them again.

Not empty.

Full.

Elara became aware of everything at once.

The heat pressing against her skin.

The faint movement of the breeze lifting the edge of her hair.

The distant sound of voices, muted by the space they occupied.

The presence of the camels behind him.

And him.

She should step back.

She knew that.

She didn't.

"What do you mean?" she asked.

His gaze held hers.

"You do not look like someone who belongs to your own world."

The words landed harder than she expected.

It wasn't an insult.

It wasn't even unkind.

It was… accurate.

Elara let out a small breath.

"That's a strange thing to say to someone you don't know."

"I know enough," he replied.

There it was again.

That certainty.

Not arrogance.

Not assumption.

Something quieter.

More grounded.

"And what is it you think you know?" she asked.

He studied her for a moment, as if deciding how much to say.

"You came here for a reason that is not only work," he said.

Elara felt her chest tighten.

"That's a guess," she said.

"It is not," he replied.

She held his gaze.

For a moment, she considered denying it.

Deflecting.

Turning the conversation back toward something easier.

She didn't.

"Maybe," she said.

The admission was small.

But it was enough.

Something shifted in his expression.

Not softer.

But less guarded.

"You should still be careful," he said.

There was no warning in his tone.

No threat.

Just fact.

Elara glanced past him, toward the camels.

"The stories," she said quietly. "Are they true?"

He did not answer immediately.

Instead, he followed her gaze.

"The desert keeps its own truths," he said finally.

It wasn't an answer.

But it was enough.

Elara looked back at him.

"You're not denying it."

A pause.

"No," he said.

Her breath caught slightly.

This was not a story anymore.

"And you're part of it," she said.

The words felt heavier than anything she had said so far.

Another pause.

Longer this time.

When he looked back at her, there was something different in his eyes.

Not defensive.

Not apologetic.

Certain.

"Yes."

The honesty of it unsettled her more than denial would have.

She should leave.

She knew that now.

Not as a suggestion.

As a fact.

But her feet didn't move.

Instead, she took a small step closer.

"Why?" she asked.

The question was not about the camels.

Not really.

It was about him.

And something in her already knew she would not be satisfied with the answer.

CHAPTER SEVEN

What He Sees

The question lingered between them.

Why.

Elara felt it settle into the space as if it had weight. Not a question asked lightly. Not something she expected him to answer easily.

Arjun did not respond immediately.

He turned slightly, his hand resting once again along the neck of the camel beside him. The animal shifted beneath his touch, then stilled, its long lashes lowering as if it understood the quiet command in his presence.

He watched the horizon for a moment.

Not avoiding her.

Considering.

"You ask like you believe there is a simple answer," he said.

His voice was calm.

Measured.

Elara crossed her arms lightly, more to steady herself than to create distance.

"There usually isn't," she said.

A faint trace of something moved through his expression.

Not quite a smile.

But close.

"Then why ask?"

She hesitated.

Because she did not have a clean answer for that either.

Because she was not sure if she was asking about the camels, the desert, the smuggling, or him.

"Because I don't understand it," she said finally.

He nodded once.

"That is honest."

The acknowledgment surprised her.

It felt… grounding.

"I could tell you it is about money," he continued. "That is part of it. Everything here has a price. Every animal. Every deal. Every man."

He glanced at her then.

"But that is not the reason."

Elara stepped slightly closer without realizing she had moved.

"Then what is?"

He let out a slow breath, his gaze returning to the camel, his fingers pressing lightly into its coarse fur.

"Some things are not chosen," he said. "They are inherited."

The word settled heavily.

Inherited.

"My family has worked with these animals for generations," he continued. "We know the desert. We know the routes. We know what survives and what does not."

Elara listened carefully.

"And at some point," he said, "the work changes."

"How?" she asked.

He looked back at her.

"You do not ask what the desert offers," he said. "You take what it gives."

The answer was not clean.

But it was clear enough.

Elara let the silence sit for a moment.

"And you're okay with that?" she asked.

There it was.

The edge.

The question she had not meant to ask so directly.

Arjun's gaze sharpened slightly.

"Do you always ask questions like this?" he said.

She held his gaze.

"Yes."

Another pause.

"Even when you know you may not like the answer?"

She felt something shift in her chest.

"Especially then."

That time, the hint of a smile reached his eyes.

Gone almost as quickly as it appeared.

"You are not afraid," he said.

It was not a compliment.

Not entirely.

Elara let out a quiet breath.

"You're wrong," she said.

He tilted his head slightly.

"Then what are you afraid of?"

The question landed harder than she expected.

Because the answer came immediately.

Not the desert.

Not the men.

Not the danger she barely understood.

Herself.

She looked away briefly, the heat rising along her skin.

"Not this," she said, gesturing lightly around them.

He watched her.

Waiting.

"Not here."

It was not a full answer.

But it was honest enough.

Arjun studied her for a moment longer.

"You are different here," he said.

Elara let out a soft laugh.

"I think it's pretty obvious that I don't belong here."

He shook his head.

"That is not what I mean."

She looked at him again.

"Then what do you mean?"

His gaze held hers, steady and unflinching.

"You are not trying to be something else here," he said. "You are not performing."

The words settled slowly.

"In your world," he continued, "you are watched in a different way."

New York flashed through her mind.

Crowded rooms. Polished conversations. The subtle, constant awareness of how she was perceived. How she presented herself. Who she needed to be in any given moment.

"And here?" she asked.

He glanced around them.

At the sand.

At the camels.

At the men moving in quiet, controlled patterns.

"Here," he said, "you are simply seen."

The difference was immediate.

And undeniable.

Elara felt it.

In New York, she had been part of a performance she barely noticed anymore.

Here, there was no performance.

Only presence.

"And you?" she asked quietly. "Are you different here?"

Arjun did not hesitate.

"No."

The certainty of it struck her.

"This is who I am," he said.

No apology.

No explanation.

Just truth.

Elara looked at him more carefully now.

Not through the lens of attraction.

Not through the curiosity that had pulled her back to this part of the fair.

But clearly.

He was not pretending.

He was not trying to be understood.

He was not offering her a version of himself that was easier to accept.

He was simply… there.

And somehow, that made him more dangerous than Luca had ever been.

Because Luca had been chaos.

Loud.

Unpredictable.

Easy to recognize as something she should walk away from.

Arjun was something else entirely.

Still.

Certain.

Rooted in a world she did not understand.

"You should go back," he said suddenly.

The words cut through the moment.

Elara blinked.

"What?"

"To the other side of the fair," he said. "To your work."

There was no dismissal in it.

No rejection.

Only distance.

"Why?" she asked.

He met her gaze one last time.

"Because this is not where your story belongs."

The words hit her harder than anything he had said.

She felt it immediately.

The resistance.

The pull.

"You don't get to decide that," she said.

Her voice was steady.

But something beneath it had sharpened.

Arjun held her gaze.

"No," he said. "But I can see it."

Silence stretched between them again.

Elara's pulse shifted.

He was wrong.

He had to be.

Because the part of her that had brought her here…

that had pushed for this assignment…

that had stepped beyond the safe edges of the fair…

That part of her was not ready to turn back.

Not now.

Not when something in her had just begun to wake up.

"I think you're wrong," she said quietly.

For a moment, neither of them moved.

Then, slowly, Arjun stepped back.

"Then you will learn," he said.

It was not a challenge.

Not quite.

But it felt like one.

Elara stood there a moment longer, watching him, trying to read something more in his expression.

But there was nothing else.

Only that same quiet certainty.

Finally, she turned.

Not because she wanted to.

Because she knew if she didn't, she might stay.

And she wasn't ready to understand what that would mean.

As she walked back toward the louder parts of the fair, the sounds returned gradually.

Voices rising.

Laughter.

The familiar rhythm of movement.

But something inside her remained altered.

Because now she knew.

This wasn't just curiosity anymore.

It was choice.

And for the first time…

she was fully aware of the direction she was choosing.

CHAPTER EIGHT

The Night Desert

She told herself she wasn't going to go back.

Not tonight.

Not after what he had said.

Not after the way he had looked at her, as if he could already see the outcome of something she hadn't yet decided.

The camp was quieter after dark.

Lanterns flickered along the paths, their soft golden light casting shadows that moved with the breeze. The air had cooled, but the warmth of the day still lingered beneath the surface, rising from the sand in faint waves.

Somewhere nearby, music played softly.

Low. Rhythmic. Almost hypnotic.

Voices drifted through the night, softer now, more relaxed. Guests moved between tents. Laughter rose and fell. Plates clinked. Glasses touched.

It should have been enough.

It wasn't.

Elara sat outside her tent for a long time, her camera resting beside her, untouched.

She tried to stay present.

Tried to focus on the glow of the lanterns. The scent of dinner still lingering in the air. The faint sweetness of something burning slowly in the distance.

But her mind kept pulling her back.

To him.

To the way he had said her name.

To the way he had seen her.

You do not look like someone who belongs to your own world.

She should have been annoyed by that.

Dismissive.

She wasn't.

The music shifted.

A deeper tone now.

Something slower.

More primal.

And before she allowed herself to think it through…

she stood.

The decision didn't feel reckless.

It felt inevitable.

The path beyond the camp was darker now.

The lanterns didn't reach this far.

The sand shifted differently beneath her feet, cooler on the surface, still holding heat beneath it. The air carried fewer scents now. Less food. Less spice.

More earth.

More night.

The fair had changed.

What had been expansive and alive during the day had condensed into something quieter.

Tighter.

The sounds were still there, but lower. Conversations happened closer together. Movements were more deliberate. The wide openness of the day had given way to something more concealed.

More intentional.

Elara walked slowly.

More aware now.

Not just of where she was going…

but of the fact that she should not be there.

Her heart beat harder.

Not from fear exactly.

From something sharper.

She moved past the familiar sections first.

The decorated camels now dimly lit, their colors muted in the low light. The working camels quieter, resting, their shapes heavy and still against the sand.

And then…

the shift.

The air changed again.

The section Ravi had warned her about felt different at night.

Not just quieter.

More controlled.

The camels stood further apart.

The men spoke less.

And the darkness itself seemed to hold more weight.

Elara stopped.

She could turn back.

She should turn back.

Instead…

she took one more step forward.

"Elara."

The sound of her name hit her instantly.

Sharper this time.

She turned.

He was already moving toward her.

Arjun Rathore.

There was no stillness in him now.

No calm distance.

His stride was purposeful. Direct. The control she had seen during the day replaced by something else entirely.

Something closer to anger.

"What are you doing here?" he said.

His voice was low.

But it wasn't calm.

Elara held her ground.

"I came back."

He stopped a few feet from her.

Too close.

Too intense.

"That is obvious," he said. "Why?"

The question wasn't curious.

It was sharp.

She felt it immediately.

The difference.

"You don't get to ask me that," she said.

His jaw tightened.

"This is not a place for you at night."

The words came harder now.

Controlled, but just barely.

"I was here earlier," she said.

"That was not the same."

The tension between them shifted.

Not playful.

Not curious.

Something else.

"Then explain it to me," she said. "Because no one else will."

For a moment, he just looked at her.

Really looked.

"You should not have come alone," he said.

There it was.

Not anger for the sake of it.

Concern.

Elara felt it land somewhere deeper than she expected.

"I'm not afraid," she said.

His expression darkened slightly.

"That is not something to be proud of."

The words cut.

Not cruelly.

Truthfully.

"You don't know me," she said.

"I know enough."

The same words.

But different now.

Heavier.

A breeze moved through the space between them, lifting the edge of her hair, carrying with it the faintest trace of something bitter.

Not spice.

Not food.

Something else.

Elara became aware of the silence around them.

Not complete silence.

But the absence of noise she had grown used to.

The absence of distraction.

"This place changes at night," he said.

His voice had lowered again.

But the intensity hadn't left.

"How?" she asked.

He took a step closer.

"During the day, people see what they expect to see," he said. "Animals. Trade. Color. Movement."

Another step.

"At night…"

He paused.

"…people do not want to be seen."

The words settled heavily between them.

Elara felt it.

The truth of it.

"And you're still here," she said.

His gaze held hers.

"Yes."

No explanation.

No justification.

"You should go back," he said again.

This time, it wasn't a suggestion.

Elara didn't move.

"Why do you care?" she asked.

The question slipped out before she could soften it.

Silence.

For a moment, she thought he wouldn't answer.

Then—

"Because you don't understand what you are walking into."

The honesty of it hit harder than anger would have.

"And you do?" she asked.

His expression didn't change.

"Yes."

Something in her shifted again.

This wasn't Luca.

This wasn't chaos.

This wasn't someone pulling her into something reckless without thought.

This was someone who knew exactly what the risk was…

and didn't want her in it.

And somehow…

that pulled her closer.

"You're not going to make me leave," she said quietly.

His eyes didn't leave hers.

"No," he said. "I am not."

A pause.

"But you will."

The certainty in his voice unsettled her more than anything else.

Because part of her knew he was right.

And part of her…

didn't want to be.

They stood there for a moment longer.

The space between them charged with something that was no longer just curiosity.

No longer just attraction.

Something deeper.

More complicated.

More dangerous.

Finally, Elara took a step back.

Not because she wanted to.

Because she understood something had shifted.

"This isn't over," she said.

It wasn't a threat.

Not quite.

Arjun watched her.

"No," he said quietly. "It is not."

And this time…

it didn't feel like a warning.

It felt like a promise.

CHAPTER NINE

What He Allows

She did not go back to the decorated section.

That was what she told herself as she dressed, as she took her tea, as she adjusted the cloth around her waist with more care than the day before. She said it the way people say things they have already decided to stop believing.

She went anyway.

The fair was different in the morning. Quieter in its commerce, louder in its preparation. Men moved with direction rather than display. Camels were led rather than exhibited. The whole place had rolled up its performance and replaced it with work.

Elara felt more at ease in it.

She moved through the outer rows without her camera raised, letting herself watch without the frame. A man repacking a saddle blanket. Two boys arguing in low voices over a rope. A vendor counting notes into a cloth pouch, his lips moving silently.

She had almost convinced herself she was simply observing.

Then she heard the voices.

Two men. Positioned behind a stack of feed sacks near the edge of the working section. They spoke quietly, but the language was fast and clipped, and though she understood none of it, the tone was unmistakable.

Displeasure.

Negotiation turning hard.

One of the men glanced up.

Elara looked away immediately, adjusting her scarf as if that were all she had been doing. She moved left, slowly, without urgency, the way Ravi had taught her without meaning to — that stillness is less visible than hurry.

Her heart was going too fast.

She didn't know what she had heard. Probably nothing. Probably ordinary trade, ordinary friction, the kind of tense exchange that happened in any market anywhere in the world.

But her body had already decided otherwise.

She turned toward the nearest open path and walked.

"Looking for something?"

She stopped.

Arjun stood a short distance behind her, his posture relaxed, his expression not.

"No," she said. Then, more honestly: "Maybe."

He studied her face for a moment.

"You heard something."

It wasn't a question.

"Two men, behind the feed sacks. I didn't understand it. I wasn't—" She stopped. "I wasn't trying to."

Arjun's jaw shifted slightly. He looked past her, toward the sacks, then back.

"Walk with me," he said.

Not an invitation.

She walked.

He moved at a pace that appeared unhurried — anyone watching would have seen a man simply moving through the fair, a woman beside him — but she felt the direction of it. Away from the voices. Into a different section. Into visibility.

"You came back," he said, when they had put enough space between themselves and the sacks.

"Yes."

"You should not have."

The words were quieter than they had been the night before.

"And yet," she said, "you didn't stop me."

Something moved through his expression.

"No."

"Why not?"

He slowed, stopping beside a row of resting camels. He looked at her for a long moment before answering.

"Because you would not have listened. And because—" He paused. "You already chose to come here."

The words landed deeper than she expected.

He wasn't talking about the walk that morning.

"What did I just hear?" she asked quietly.

His eyes didn't move from hers.

"Nothing that concerns you."

"It concerned me enough to make me walk away from it."

"Yes." He looked at her steadily. "That was the right thing to do."

"I want to know what it was."

"I know you do."

The simplicity of it shut the conversation down in a way that more words could not have. It wasn't a door closed. It was a door that had never been open.

Elara looked away, toward the camels.

"So this is it," she said. "This is the part no one talks about."

"This is the part people pretend does not exist."

"And yet it does."

"Yes."

The silence that followed was fuller than their words. Around them, the fair continued — voices, movement, negotiation — but it seemed distant now, as if they stood slightly outside of it.

"I'm not sending you away," he said finally.

"But you're not going to tell me anything."

"No."

She turned back to him.

"Then show me what you can."

He held her gaze for a long moment. The morning light moved across his face and told her nothing.

Then, without another word, he turned and began to walk.

Not away.

Forward.

Elara hesitated only briefly.

Then followed.

And as she stepped behind him, she felt the line she had been approaching since she arrived move not beneath her feet, but somewhere deeper.

She had already crossed it.

She just hadn't admitted it until now.

CHAPTER TEN

What Is Not Meant to Be Seen

He did not look back to see if she followed.

He didn't need to.

Elara walked a few steps behind him, matching his pace without fully realizing she had adjusted to it. The sand shifted beneath her feet more deeply here, less traveled, less compacted by the movement of crowds. The air felt different too.

Still warm.

Still carrying the faint trace of dust and animal.

But quieter.

Contained.

The sounds of the fair softened behind them.

Voices faded.

Laughter disappeared.

Even the bells tied to the decorated camels seemed distant now, their soft chimes replaced by something more muted.

Arjun moved with certainty.

Not quickly.

Not slowly.

But with the kind of awareness that came from knowing exactly where he was and what surrounded him at all times.

Elara noticed the way others responded to him.

They did not greet him.

They did not call out.

But they moved.

Subtly.

Space opened where he walked. Conversations lowered as he passed. A glance here. A nod there. A quiet acknowledgment that did not require words.

Respect.

Or something close to it.

She adjusted her camera slightly against her shoulder, though she had not lifted it since following him.

This did not feel like a place for photographs.

Not yet.

They reached a small rise in the sand, just enough to overlook part of the section below. Arjun stopped there, his gaze moving across the space with quiet precision.

Elara stopped beside him.

From here, she could see more clearly.

The camels were arranged differently in this area.

Further apart.

Positioned with intention rather than convenience.

Some stood tethered.

Others were not.

But none wandered.

"They are trained," she said softly.

Arjun didn't look at her.

"Yes."

"For what?"

A pause.

"For obedience," he said.

The word settled differently here.

Heavier.

Elara watched one of the camels shift its weight, its body still, its head lifted as if listening to something beyond what she could hear.

"They don't seem afraid," she said.

"They are not," he replied.

"Then what keeps them here?"

That time, he turned slightly.

"Understanding."

She frowned.

"Of what?"

He held her gaze for a moment.

"Of what happens if they do not return."

The answer sent a quiet chill through her.

Before she could respond, movement below caught her attention.

A group of older men had gathered near one of the camels.

They stood close together, their conversation low, their expressions unreadable from where she stood. One of them turned slightly, his gaze lifting.

Toward them.

Elara felt it immediately.

Not curiosity.

Awareness.

The man said something to the others.

They did not turn fully.

But their posture shifted.

Subtle.

Controlled.

"They see you," Arjun said quietly.

Elara didn't look away.

"I assumed they would."

"That is not what I mean."

She glanced at him.

"They see you coming here," he said. "More than once."

The weight of that settled in.

"And that's a problem?" she asked.

He didn't answer right away.

Instead, he watched the men below, his expression tightening just slightly.

"Yes."

The simplicity of it was enough.

"Why?" she pressed.

This time, when he turned to her, there was something different in his eyes.

Less guarded.

More direct.

"Because they are not interested in your photographs," he said.

The words were quiet.

But sharp.

"They are interested in what does not belong."

Elara felt her breath catch slightly.

"And I don't belong," she said.

It wasn't a question.

"No," he said.

Another pause.

"And neither does this."

His gaze dropped briefly between them.

Elara followed it.

The space.

The distance.

The way they stood beside each other as if it were natural.

As if it had already become something.

Something visible.

Her chest tightened.

"You think they're watching us," she said.

"I know they are."

The certainty in his voice left no room for doubt.

Elara looked back toward the men.

One of them shifted slightly, his gaze no longer directly on her, but not fully turned away either.

A warning.

Unspoken.

"Why does it matter?" she asked.

Arjun's jaw tightened.

"Because this is not a place where things like this happen," he said.

"Things like what?"

He didn't answer immediately.

Instead, he stepped closer.

Just enough to remove the distance between them.

"This," he said quietly.

The word barely moved through the air.

Elara felt it more than she heard it.

Her pulse shifted.

There was no mistaking it now.

They had crossed something.

Not physically.

Not yet.

But clearly.

"And what exactly is this?" she asked.

Her voice was softer now.

He held her gaze.

"A mistake," he said.

The word landed harder than she expected.

She felt it instantly.

That familiar tension.

The push and pull.

The part of her that recognized the truth.

And the part of her that resisted it.

"You don't know that," she said.

His expression didn't change.

"I do."

The same certainty.

The same quiet conviction.

Elara let out a slow breath.

"And yet you brought me here," she said.

Another pause.

"I did not bring you," he said. "You followed."

She almost smiled.

"That's a technicality."

For the first time, something close to real amusement touched his expression.

Gone quickly.

But there.

"It is not," he said.

Silence settled again.

The men below began to disperse slowly, but the awareness remained.

The space around them still held weight.

Still held attention.

Elara looked back at Arjun.

"Then why didn't you stop me?" she asked.

The question came quieter this time.

More honest.

He held her gaze for a long moment.

"Because I wanted to see if you would come back," he said.

The truth of it hit her instantly.

"And now that I have?"

A pause.

His expression shifted.

Not softer.

Not harder.

Something more complicated.

"Now I know," he said.

Her breath caught.

"Knew what?"

He looked at her fully then.

No distance.

No deflection.

"That you will not walk away easily."

The words settled deep.

Because they weren't just about this place.

They were about her.

And she knew it.

Elara felt something rise in her chest.

Recognition.

Resistance.

Something dangerously close to acceptance.

Behind them, the wind shifted again, carrying dust lightly across the sand.

The fair moved on.

The men dispersed.

The camels stood.

But the space between them remained.

Charged.

Watched.

And no longer something that could be ignored.

CHAPTER ELEVEN

What She Came For

She didn't go back to him that afternoon.

Not because she didn't want to.

Because she knew she shouldn't.

The separation felt unnatural.

Like pulling herself out of something mid-thought.

Incomplete.

Elara walked back through the fair slowly, the sounds returning in layers as she moved away from the quieter section. Voices rose again. Laughter cut through the air. Bells chimed softly as decorated camels shifted their weight beneath bright fabrics and intricate patterns.

The world she was supposed to be documenting.

She stopped.

Stood still for a moment.

And let herself remember why she had come.

The camera rested against her chest.

Familiar.

Grounding.

This is what you do.

The thought came clearly this time.

Not emotional.

Not complicated.

Just true.

Elara lifted the camera.

And everything shifted.

The noise softened.

Not because it disappeared.

Because she filtered it.

The lens framed the world into something intentional.

Controlled.

Click.

A man leading two camels across a narrow stretch of sand, his shadow long behind him, stretching toward the fading light.

Click.

A group of traders seated close together, their hands moving as they negotiated, their expressions sharp, focused, alive with quiet intensity.

Click.

A young boy standing beside a decorated camel, his hand resting lightly against its side, his gaze fixed somewhere beyond the crowd.

She adjusted her position.

Changed her angle.

Lowered herself slightly to catch the light differently as it shifted across the sand.

Click.

This was her language.

Not conversation.

Not explanation.

Observation.

She moved deeper into the busier sections, letting herself disappear again in the movement. Here, she could blend more easily. The attention that had followed her earlier softened. She became part of the background again.

A presence.

Not a disruption.

The smells returned stronger in this part of the fair.

Food being prepared in open pans.

Oil heating.

Spices blooming in the heat.

Turmeric.

Cumin.

Chili.

The air carried sweetness too. Something fried and soaked in syrup. Sticky. Rich. Almost too sweet, yet impossible to ignore.

Elara paused near a food stall, lifting her camera again.

Click.

Steam rising from a pan, catching the light in soft curls.

Click.

A hand reaching into a bowl of bright orange sweets, lifting one carefully before placing it onto a plate.

She lowered the camera and took a breath.

This was what her editor would expect.

Color.

Texture.

Life.

But something felt different now.

She noticed it slowly.

Her eye wasn't settling the way it usually did.

The shots were good.

Strong.

Clean.

But they weren't enough.

Because now she had seen something else.

The quieter section.

The controlled movement.

The men who spoke less.

The camels that stood differently.

Him.

Elara adjusted her grip on the camera.

No.

She forced herself back into the moment.

Focus.

She moved toward a group of traders, positioning herself just outside their circle. She waited. Watched. Let the moment build instead of taking it immediately.

A man leaned forward.

Another responded.

Their hands met briefly.

Click.

The deal was done.

She exhaled slowly.

That was the shot.

The kind of image that told a story without explanation.

She checked the screen briefly.

Sharp.

Perfectly framed.

Light hitting at just the right angle.

This is why they sent you.

The thought grounded her.

Not because she had asked for the assignment.

Because she had earned it.

Elara lowered the camera again, letting it rest against her chest.

And still…

something pulled.

She turned slightly, her gaze drifting across the fair without intention.

And there it was.

The edge.

The place where the movement changed.

Where the sound thinned.

Where the story shifted from visible to hidden.

Her breath caught slightly.

Even from this distance, she could feel it.

And without thinking…

she lifted the camera again.

But this time, she didn't step forward.

She stayed where she was.

And zoomed.

The lens stretched across the distance, narrowing the space between her and the section she had left behind.

The frame settled.

A man standing beside a camel.

Still.

Watching.

Click.

She adjusted slightly.

Focused.

And then—

He stepped into the frame.

Arjun.

Not looking at her.

Not acknowledging her.

But present.

The shot caught him in motion.

His hand resting briefly along the camel's neck.

His gaze turned slightly away.

His posture composed, controlled, unbothered by the world around him.

Elara held the camera steady.

Something shifted in her chest.

Click.

The image stayed on the screen for a moment longer than the others.

Not because it was technically better.

Because it meant something.

She lowered the camera slowly.

This was not part of the assignment.

And yet…

it felt like the most important photograph she had taken all day.

Elara stood there a moment longer, her gaze fixed on the distance.

Then, deliberately…

She turned away.

Not because the pull had disappeared.

Because she understood it now.

And understanding it didn't make it weaker.

It made it clearer.

CHAPTER TWELVE

The Photograph

She knew he had seen her.

Not in the moment.

Not when she had lifted the camera and framed him from across the fair.

But later.

It was the kind of knowing that did not come from evidence.

It came from instinct.

Elara sat on the low step outside her tent as the afternoon softened into evening, her camera resting in her lap.

She had gone back through the images once.

Then again.

Slower the second time.

More deliberate.

The photographs from earlier in the day were strong.

Exactly what they needed to be.

Color.

Movement.

Story.

She could already see how they would lay out across the pages of a magazine.

A wide shot of the fair stretching into the distance.

A close frame of a trader's hands.

A child's face caught between curiosity and stillness.

It was all there.

And yet…

Her thumb paused on the screen.

That image.

Him.

She studied it again.

It wasn't posed.

It wasn't even aware of her.

That was what made it different.

His hand resting against the camel's neck.

The slight turn of his head.

The stillness in his posture.

There was no performance in it.

No effort.

It was simply him.

Elara felt something shift in her chest.

This wasn't just a photograph.

It was something she had taken.

Without asking.

Without permission.

The thought stayed with her longer than she expected.

The light faded further, the sky softening into muted tones of gold and pale rose before slipping toward dusk.

Lanterns were being lit again along the paths, their glow returning warmth to the edges of the camp.

The air cooled.

The scent of food drifted back in, richer now.

Spiced lentils.

Roasted vegetables.

Something sweet again, heavier this time.

Elara stood slowly.

She hadn't decided to go.

Not consciously.

And yet…

Her feet carried her forward.

The path beyond the camp felt familiar now.

Not comfortable.

Not safe.

But known.

The fair at dusk existed somewhere between day and night.

The louder sections still held energy, voices rising and falling, but the edges had begun to quiet.

Shadows lengthened.

Movement slowed.

Elara walked carefully.

More aware now of how she entered each space.

How she moved.

How she was seen.

When she reached the outer edge of the quieter section, she didn't step in immediately.

She waited.

As if giving herself the chance to turn back.

She didn't.

"You came again."

The voice came from behind her.

Not sharp.

Not surprised.

Certain.

Elara turned.

Arjun stood a few steps away, his posture relaxed, his expression unreadable in the dimming light.

"I didn't think you'd be surprised," she said.

"I am not," he replied.

Silence settled between them.

He studied her for a moment longer than usual.

Not casually.

Not curiously.

Intentionally.

"You were taking photographs today," he said.

It wasn't a question.

Elara felt the shift immediately.

"Yes."

Another pause.

"You took one of me."

The words landed softly.

But precisely.

There was no accusation in his tone.

That made it worse.

Elara held his gaze.

"Yes."

No explanation.

No apology.

Just truth.

For a moment, neither of them moved.

Then he took a step closer.

"Why?"

The question was quieter now.

More personal.

Elara felt the weight of it.

She could have answered easily.

Deflected.

Said something about composition, light, storytelling.

She didn't.

"Because you were part of the story," she said.

His gaze sharpened slightly.

"No," he said. "I am not."

The certainty in his voice struck her.

"You are," she replied, just as steady.

Another pause.

"This is not your story," he said.

The words carried more weight now.

Elara felt something rise in her chest.

"It is while I'm here," she said.

That time, something shifted in his expression.

Not anger.

Something closer to conflict.

"You do not understand what you are doing," he said.

The words were familiar.

But the tone was different.

Quieter.

More contained.

"And you do?" she asked.

A small breath.

"Yes."

The honesty of it settled between them again.

Elara reached into her bag without breaking eye contact.

Slowly.

Carefully.

She pulled out the camera.

His gaze dropped briefly to it.

Then back to her.

"Do you want to see it?" she asked.

The question surprised both of them.

A long pause followed.

Then, finally—

"Yes."

She stepped closer.

Close enough now that she could feel the heat still held in the air between them.

Close enough that the distance between them no longer felt like space.

Elara turned the camera slightly, bringing the image up on the screen.

For a moment, neither of them spoke.

He looked at it.

Not quickly.

Not dismissively.

Carefully.

As if he were trying to understand something beyond the image itself.

Elara watched him.

Not the photograph.

Him.

"What do you see?" she asked quietly.

Another pause.

"Someone who should not be in your frame," he said.

The answer was immediate.

Elara felt it land.

"That's not what I see," she said.

He looked up at her.

"What do you see?" he asked.

She held his gaze.

"Someone who doesn't pretend," she said.

The words came softer than she expected.

But they were true.

Something shifted in his expression again.

Not visible to anyone else.

But she saw it.

"You think that is a good thing," he said.

"I think it's rare," she replied.

Silence.

The air between them felt different now.

Less guarded.

More exposed.

"You should not keep this," he said.

Her fingers tightened slightly around the camera.

"Why?"

Another pause.

"Because it makes something real," he said.

The words settled deeper than anything else he had said.

Elara felt it immediately.

This wasn't about the photograph.

It was about what it meant.

She lowered the camera slowly.

"It already is," she said.

Their eyes held.

Longer this time.

And for the first time since she had met him…

The distance between them didn't feel like protection.

It felt like something waiting to be crossed.

CHAPTER THIRTEEN

The Space Between Words

They didn't move right away.

After the photograph.

After the words that lingered longer than either of them had expected.

The fair continued around them, but it felt distant now.

Muted.

Like something happening behind glass.

Elara became aware of the closeness first.

Not sudden.

Not overwhelming.

Just present.

The space between them had narrowed without either of them fully acknowledging it. Close enough that she could see the subtle details she had missed before.

The faint line along his jaw where the sun had caught him too often.

The way his eyes held stillness, but not emptiness.

There was something beneath it.

Something contained.

She should step back.

She knew that.

She didn't.

Arjun shifted slightly, his gaze moving past her for a moment, scanning the edge of the space as if checking something unseen.

Then back to her.

"You should not stay here long," he said.

His voice had softened again.

Not distant.

Not cold.

Measured.

"I've heard that before," she replied. .

A faint trace of something moved through his expression.

Not quite amusement.

But close enough.

"You do not listen," he said.

Elara let out a small breath.

"No," she said. "I just don't always agree."

Silence settled between them again.

This time, it felt less tense.

Less guarded.

More… open.

Arjun looked at her more carefully now.

Not assessing.

Not evaluating.

Seeing.

"You ask questions," he said.

It wasn't new.

But the way he said it was.

"And you don't like that?" she asked.

Another small pause.

"I did not say that."

She studied him for a moment.

"What don't you like?" she asked quietly.

The question shifted something.

She felt it immediately.

He didn't answer right away.

Instead, he looked away.

Not dismissing her.

Thinking.

"When people come here," he said slowly, "they see what they want to see."

Elara listened.

"They see color. Movement. Something different from their own lives," he continued. "They take photographs. They leave."

The words were simple.

But not empty.

"And you?" she asked.

His gaze returned to hers.

"You look longer," he said.

The statement landed softly.

But it carried weight.

"You stay where others don't," he added.

Elara felt that.

"And that's a problem?" she asked.

Another pause.

"It can be."

The honesty of it didn't feel like warning this time.

It felt like truth.

She shifted her weight slightly, the sand pressing differently beneath her feet.

"I'm not here to take something and leave," she said.

The words came before she could soften them.

Arjun's expression changed.

Not dramatically.

But enough.

"That is exactly what you will do," he said.

The certainty in his voice struck her.

"You don't know that," she said.

"I do."

The same quiet conviction.

The same grounded certainty that made arguing with him feel… pointless.

And yet—

"You don't know me," she said.

That time, he didn't answer immediately.

He held her gaze for a long moment.

Long enough that the space between them felt different again.

"I know enough," he said.

The words were quieter now.

Not dismissive.

Not final.

Something else.

Elara felt something shift in her chest.

"What do you think you know?" she asked.

This time, when he answered, there was no hesitation.

"That you do not stay anywhere long," he said.

The words landed cleanly.

Directly.

Elara felt it instantly.

Because it was true.

She opened her mouth to respond.

Stopped.

Closed it again.

Arjun watched her carefully.

Not with satisfaction.

Not with judgment.

Recognition.

"You see things clearly," he said. "But you do not stay long enough for them to matter."

The statement cut deeper than she expected.

Because it wasn't about the fair.

It wasn't about the camels.

It was about her.

Her throat tightened slightly.

"That's not fair," she said.

His expression didn't change.

"No," he said. "It is not."

Silence stretched again.

Elara felt the familiar instinct rise.

To deflect.

To pull away.

To turn the moment into something lighter, easier, less exposed.

She didn't.

"Maybe I haven't found something worth staying for," she said.

The words came softer than she intended.

Honest.

And for the first time since she had met him…

Something in Arjun shifted in a way she couldn't ignore.

It was small.

Barely visible.

But it was there.

A crack.

Gone almost immediately.

But real.

He looked at her then, fully.

No distance.

No deflection.

"That is not the same thing," he said.

His voice had changed.

Lower.

And something in it felt…

different.

Elara felt it.

The shift.

This wasn't just observation anymore.

This was something closer to… understanding.

Or maybe something he didn't want to understand.

The air between them felt heavier now.

Not tense.

Not fragile.

Something deeper.

Elara became aware of her own breathing.

Slower.

More deliberate.

"You think I leave because I want to," she said.

Another pause.

"I think you leave because you can," he replied.

The words landed differently.

Not as an accusation.

As fact.

Elara felt something rise again.

Not defensiveness.

Something else.

Recognition.

Because he wasn't wrong.

She had always left.

Before things became complicated.

Before they became real.

Before they required something she wasn't sure she knew how to give.

The realization settled quietly.

And for a moment…

she didn't know what to say.

Arjun watched her.

Then, without warning…

He stepped back.

The distance returned.

Just enough.

"We should not be standing like this," he said.

The words felt different now.

Not just caution.

Control.

Something being pulled back into place.

Elara felt it immediately.

The moment closing.

The space shifting again.

"Why?" she asked.

The question came softer now.

Less defiant.

He held her gaze one last time.

"Because it becomes something else," he said.

The words settled between them.

Clear.

Unavoidable.

Elara didn't respond.

Because she understood.

And that understanding didn't make it easier.

It made it harder.

Arjun turned then.

Not abruptly.

Not dismissively.

But deliberately.

And began to walk away.

This time…

she didn't follow.

She stood there, watching him move back into the space he belonged to.

The space she did not.

And for the first time…

She felt the distance not as separation.

But as something that had already begun to matter.

CHAPTER FOURTEEN

The Edge of Knowing

The fair felt different that day.

Not quieter. Not calmer. If anything, it was louder — more crowded, more alive — but something beneath the surface had shifted. Elara felt it the moment she stepped off the red carpet and into the open expanse of sand.

The air carried more dust, lifted by a steady wind that moved through the rows of camels and people like something searching. Voices rose in bursts — laughter, bargaining, arguments that seemed to dissolve as quickly as they formed. The bells tied around the camels' necks chimed irregularly, creating a rhythm that never quite settled.

Everything was in motion.

Everything except her.

Ravi had warned her that morning before she could ask.

"Decisions being made today," he said, without preamble. "Movement. Things that should not be photographed."

"How will I know what those things are?"

He looked at her. "You will feel it. A picture that costs you something before you take it — do not take that one."

She had nodded, meaning it.

She had meant it for almost three hours.

The photograph happened by accident. Or so she told herself afterward.

She had been framing a shot of the working camels — the lean ones, the unbelled ones, the ones that stood apart from the fair's theater — when movement in her peripheral vision made her adjust the lens. Two men. A third emerging from behind them. A package changed hands so briefly she almost missed it.

Almost.

Her shutter fired before she had made the decision.

One frame.

She lowered the camera immediately, her pulse spiking.

No one had seen her.

Or so she thought.

She moved left, slowly, the way she'd learned — stillness is less visible than hurry. She put three rows of camels between herself and the men without appearing to.

Then she stopped, pressed her back against the flank of a resting animal, and waited.

Nothing happened.

After a minute, she exhaled.

After two, she convinced herself it was fine.

"Why do you hesitate?"

She turned.

Arjun stood there. He hadn't approached loudly. Hadn't called out. He was simply there now, as if the space had allowed him to exist within it without announcement.

Her breath caught — just slightly.

"I don't," she said.

He watched her for a moment. Then glanced at the camera in her hand.

"You do."

Elara followed his gaze, then looked back at him.

"I'm choosing."

"Show me."

"What?"

"What you've taken today."

The request was quiet. The certainty beneath it was not.

She felt it immediately — the pull to refuse, the separate pull to comply, and underneath both of them, the awareness that he already suspected.

She turned the camera and scrolled back.

He watched without reaching for it. When the frame appeared — the two men, the third, the package — she felt his stillness shift into something else. Something controlled very deliberately.

He said nothing for a moment.

"Delete it."

Not a request.

Elara looked at the image.

"I wasn't trying to—"

"I know what you were trying to do," he said. "Delete it anyway."

Her thumb hovered.

She deleted it.

The silence that followed was different from their usual silences. It had weight to it. Not anger — something more precise. The specific quality of a man deciding how much to say.

"You felt it before you took it," he said finally.

"Yes."

"And you took it anyway."

She didn't answer. She didn't need to.

Arjun looked out over the camels, his jaw set.

"You do not follow rules," she said.

"No." He looked back at her. "I follow consequences."

"And if someone had seen me?"

A pause.

"Then we would not be having this conversation."

The plainness of it moved through her slowly.

They stood side by side, facing the camels. Not touching. Not moving closer. But the space between them felt different now — not charged, but careful. The way a room feels after something breakable has almost fallen.

"You're different today," he said after a moment.

"So are you."

He didn't deny it.

"I won't see you tonight," he said.

The statement came without warning.

"Why?"

"There are things to do."

She looked away, toward the camels stretching into the distance.

"When will I see you again?"

He didn't answer right away.

Then, "If it happens, it happens."

"That's not an answer."

"It is the only one that matters."

She turned back to him. Part of her wanted to push. To ask more. But the image she had just deleted sat between them, and she understood, more clearly than before, that some distances were not obstacles.

They were architecture.

"Okay," she said.

He watched her closely. As if measuring something.

Then, softer: "You are learning."

She almost laughed.

"That doesn't feel like a compliment."

"It is not meant to."

He held her gaze a moment longer.

Then he was gone — not dramatically, not with distance, simply absorbed back into the fair as if he had always been part of it and her presence had been the interruption.

Elara stood alone beside the camels.

The deleted frame was gone.

The weight of it was not.

CHAPTER FIFTEEN

The Shift *(Expanded)*

She didn't go looking for him.

That was the first difference.

Elara woke before the light had fully settled across the desert, the quiet of the early morning wrapping around her in a way that felt almost deliberate. The camp had not yet fully stirred. Movement was minimal. Sound softened to its barest form.

For a moment, she stayed where she was, lying still beneath the thin woven cover, listening.

To the absence.

To the space between things.

It took her a few seconds to understand what had woken her.

Not noise.

Not movement.

Awareness.

Something had shifted inside her.

Again.

She sat up slowly, the fabric brushing softly against her skin, and moved toward the entrance of the tent. The canvas glowed faintly with the rising light, the world outside still suspended between darkness and day.

When she stepped out, the air met her gently.

Cooler than it had been in days.

Carrying only the faintest trace of scent.

Sand.

Dust.

A distant memory of smoke.

The fair was still there.

Of course it was.

But in this hour, it felt different.

Less performative.

Less layered.

Honest.

Elara stood for a moment, letting her body adjust, letting her thoughts settle into something she could follow.

He had pulled away.

Not dramatically.

Not in a way that demanded reaction.

But clearly.

And instead of pushing her back…

it had done something else.

It had stilled her.

That was new.

In New York, distance had always created movement.

Reaction.

Pursuit.

With Luca, distance had been a trigger.

The moment he pulled away, she had leaned in harder.

Tried to close the gap.

Tried to fix something that was never hers to fix.

But this…

This was different.

She didn't feel the need to chase.

She felt the need to understand.

The realization settled quietly.

And that was when she knew.

She would go back.

Not because she couldn't help it.

Because she was choosing to.

Elara dressed more slowly than usual, aware of each movement. She adjusted the cloth around her waist carefully, securing it with more intention than she had the first day. Her hair she left loose, but less carelessly.

There was no performance in it.

No attempt to become something else.

Just awareness.

When she stepped into the camp, the morning had begun to unfold. Staff moved between tents carrying trays of tea, the scent of chai returning with its familiar warmth.

Cardamom.

Ginger.

Milk.

She accepted a cup, wrapping her hands around it, letting the heat anchor her.he took a sip.

Slower this time.

Tasting it fully.

Everything here asked for that.

Presence.

Attention.

Elara moved through the early morning calmly, lifting her camera only when the moment called for it, not out of habit.

Click.

A man kneeling beside a camel, brushing its coat with careful, rhythmic movements.

Click.

A woman pouring tea into a small glass, her hands steady, precise.

She worked like that for a while.

Measured.

Intentional.

And then…

The awareness returned.

Stronger now.

She didn't resist it.

She let it settle.

Let it become part of her movement instead of something separate from it.

And only then…

She turned.

He was there.

Not hidden.

Not waiting.

Standing at a distance, exactly where she had felt him.

Their eyes met.

This time, there was no hesitation.

No surprise.

Only recognition.

Elara held his gaze for a moment longer than necessary.

Then turned away.

Not dismissing him.

Acknowledging him.

She lifted her camera again.

Click.

A line of camels crossing the light.

Click.

A trader adjusting the edge of his turban.

She moved.

Worked.

Breathed.

And then, when the moment felt right…

She lowered the camera.

And walked toward him.

Not pulled.

Choosing.

Each step grounded.

Each movement deliberate.

The shift in the air was immediate as she entered the quieter section.

The sounds softened.

The space tightened.

But this time…

it didn't feel like crossing into something forbidden.

It felt like entering something she understood.

He didn't move.

He watched her approach, his expression steady, but no longer guarded in the same way.

When she stopped in front of him, the space between them felt… balanced.

Not tense.

Not distant.

Present.

"You didn't try to stop me today," she said.

Her voice was calm.

"No."

No hesitation.

"And you're not leaving."

Another truth.

"No."

The simplicity of it settled something inside her.

Silence followed.

But it wasn't uncomfortable.

Elara shifted her weight slightly, feeling the sand beneath her feet.

"I thought about what you said," she said.

He watched her.

"What part?"

"That I don't stay," she said.

A pause.

"And?"

She let out a small breath.

"Maybe you're right."

The admission was quiet.

But real.

Something shifted in his expression.

Not victory.

Not satisfaction.

Recognition.

Elara held his gaze.

"But I'm still here," she added.

Another pause.

"Yes," he said.

"And I'm not pretending I don't want to understand this," she continued.

Her voice didn't waver.

Or you.

She didn't say it.

But it was there.

He heard it.

She knew he did.

Arjun exhaled slowly, his gaze dropping for a brief moment before returning to hers.

"You think this is something you can step into and step out of," he said.

The words were quieter now.

Less sharp.

"Maybe I did," she said.

Another pause.

"But I don't think that anymore."

The truth of it settled fully this time.

He stepped closer.

Deliberate.

Not closing the distance entirely.

But changing it.

"You should," he said.

The words felt softer now.

Almost… protective.

Elara shook her head slightly.

"I don't want to."

There it was.

Clear.

Uncomplicated.

Something shifted again.

Deeper this time.

He didn't step back.

The space held.

And for the first time…

He allowed it.

"You are making a choice you do not understand," he said.

His voice was low now.

Closer.

Elara met his gaze.

"I understand enough."

Silence.

The air between them felt different.

Heavier.

More present.

He studied her.

Not as an outsider.

Not as a risk.

As something else.

"You are not going to leave," he said.

It wasn't a question.

Elara felt it settle fully in her chest.

"Not yet."

The words came without hesitation.

Honest.

Final.

And this time…

He didn't argue.

He didn't correct her.

He didn't create distance.

Instead…

He stayed.

CHAPTER SIXTEEN

The Shape of the Day *(Expanded)*

The desert held the heat long after the sun had begun its slow descent.

Elara felt it beneath her feet as she stepped beyond the edge of the camp, the sand still warm from the day, shifting softly with each step, pressing upward as if the ground itself retained memory.

The air was different now.

Less sharp than midday.

Less forgiving than morning.

It moved more slowly, carrying with it the layered scents of the fair.

Spice.

Dust.

Animal.

Smoke that never fully disappeared.

She paused just beyond the last of the red carpets, letting her eyes adjust to the light.

Everything had softened.

Not in clarity.

In tone.

The harsh edges of the afternoon had eased into something more fluid. Shadows stretched longer across the sand. The colors deepened slightly. Gold turned warmer. Browns richer. The sky held that faint shift toward evening that came before the sun began to fall.

Elara lifted her camera, but didn't shoot.

Not yet.

She watched.

A camel shifted its weight nearby, the movement slow and deliberate, its long legs adjusting beneath its body as it turned its head slightly, exhaling a low, steady breath that carried warmth into the air.

A group of men stood not far from it, their voices low, their gestures minimal, their presence contained within a quiet understanding that didn't require volume.

This part of the fair moved differently.

Elara stepped forward, the sand rising in fine dust around her ankles, catching briefly in the light before settling again.

She could feel it now.

Not just the place.

The rhythm.

And then—

The awareness returned.

Not distant this time.

Close.

She didn't need to turn to know.

But she did anyway.

Arjun stood several paces away, his presence as steady as the ground beneath them.

He hadn't approached.

He hadn't called out.

He had simply allowed her to notice him.

The difference mattered.

Elara held his gaze for a moment, longer than she had before.

Then lowered the camera slightly.

"You stayed," she said.

Her voice carried easily in the open space.

"I told you I would."

His tone was even.

But there was something quieter in it now.

Less resistance.

Elara stepped toward him.

Not hesitating.

Not rushing.

The sand shifted beneath her feet, the fine grains slipping slightly with each step, forcing her to adjust her balance as she moved.

She became aware of the way her body moved through the space.

The way the air pressed against her skin.

The way the light caught the edges of everything.

When she reached him, she didn't stop immediately.

She moved just slightly past him.

Then turned.

So they stood side by side.

Not facing each other.

Facing the same direction.

The difference was subtle.

But it changed everything.

For a moment, neither of them spoke.

The fair stretched out in front of them, its movement constant, its sound rising and falling in waves that never fully broke.

A line of camels moved slowly across the horizon, their silhouettes elongated by the angle of the sun.

Dust lifted beneath their feet, hanging briefly in the air before dissolving into the light.

Elara lifted her camera.

Click.

The frame caught the line perfectly.

She lowered it again.

"You don't rush anything here," she said.

Arjun glanced at her.

"You cannot rush this place," he replied.

A pause.

"It does not respond to urgency."

Elara considered that.

In New York, everything responded to urgency.

Speed.

Pressure.

Momentum.

Here…

Everything waited.

She stepped forward slightly, moving down a small slope in the sand, her footing shifting more noticeably now. The ground was softer here, less compacted, each step sinking just enough to require attention.

Arjun followed without comment.

They walked like that for a while.

Not aimlessly.

But without a fixed destination.

Elara found herself noticing everything more deeply now.

The way the sand changed texture underfoot. Some areas fine and loose, others packed more firmly, shaped by repeated movement.

The way the air carried sound differently depending on where they stood. Voices clear in one moment, distant the next.

The way the camels moved with a kind of deliberate patience, never hurried, never careless.

She lifted the camera again.

Click.

A close frame this time.

A man's hand resting against the coarse fur of a camel's neck.

Click.

The texture of it.

The weight of it.

She lowered the camera and exhaled slowly.

"You see more now," Arjun said.

She glanced at him.

"Because I'm looking longer?"

He shook his head slightly.

"Because you are not trying to take it with you."

The words settled differently.

Elara felt that.

She hadn't realized it.

But he was right.

She wasn't collecting moments anymore.

She was letting them exist.

They moved further into the quieter section, the space opening slightly, the distance between people increasing.

The air felt stiller here.

More contained.

A sudden breeze moved through, lifting fine sand into the air.

Elara turned instinctively, raising her hand to shield her face as the dust brushed against her skin.

It settled along her arms, warm and soft, catching lightly in the strands of her hair.

She laughed softly.

Not out of amusement.

Out of sensation.

"It's everywhere," she said.

Arjun watched her.

"It becomes part of you," he replied.

She brushed her arm lightly, watching the dust shift but not fully disappear.

"I believe that," she said.

For a moment, they stood still.

The breeze faded.

The air settled again.

And then—

Without thinking—

He reached out.

His hand brushed along her forearm.

Slow.

Deliberate.

Not removing the dust.

Feeling it.

The contact was different this time.

Not instinctive.

Not brief.

Intentional.

Elara felt it immediately.

The warmth of his hand.

The contrast of his touch against the fine layer of sand along her skin.

Her breath shifted.

Neither of them moved. The moment stretched.

Then, slowly—

He pulled his hand back.

The space between them returned.

But it felt different now.

Closer.

Not because of distance.

Because of awareness.

Elara looked at him.

He didn't look away.

"You should not get used to this," he said.

His voice was quieter now.

She tilted her head slightly.

"To what?"

A pause.

"This."

The word held more than it said.

Elara felt it.

"I'm not trying to get used to it," she said.

Another pause.

"I'm trying to understand it."

Silence settled again.

Arjun studied her for a long moment.

Then—

"You are already inside it," he said.

The words landed softly.

But completely.

Elara felt the truth of it settle into her chest.

There was no stepping in and out anymore.

No distance she could create that would undo what had already begun.

She looked out across the desert again.

The light had shifted further now, the sun lowering, the sky beginning to deepen.

The fair moved on.

The camels shifted.

The world continued.

And yet—

Something had changed.

Not around her.

Within her.

She lowered the camera slowly.

And for the first time since she had arrived…

She didn't feel like she was documenting something temporary.

She felt like she was standing inside something that would stay with her.

Long after she left.

CHAPTER SEVENTEEN

What the Desert Hides

The light was almost gone by the time Arjun began to walk again.

Not back toward the fair.

Not toward the camp.

Away from both.

Elara noticed the direction immediately, though she said nothing at first. The space around them had begun to change. The crowd thinned behind them, voices dropping into the distance until they became less distinct, more like memory than sound. The camels nearby stood in loose clusters, their bodies darkening against the fading light, their long shadows stretching thin across the sand.

The desert opened ahead.

Wide.

Still.

Waiting.

Elara adjusted the camera strap across her shoulder and followed.

She did not ask where they were going.

Part of her knew he would not answer if she did.

Another part of her did not want the answer yet.

The sand changed beneath her feet as they moved farther from the main paths. It became softer, less marked by cart wheels and footsteps. Each step sank slightly, forcing her to move more slowly, to pay attention to the ground. Fine dust lifted around her ankles and settled along the hem of her skirt, coating the fabric in pale gold.

The air had cooled.

Not much.

Just enough to make her aware of the day leaving.

The smell of the fair faded behind them. Less oil. Less spice. Less smoke from cooking fires. Out here, the scent was simpler.

Sand.

Dry brush.

Animal.

Wind.

Arjun walked ahead of her, his pace steady but not hurried. He seemed to know the ground by instinct, where it would hold, where it would give way, where the wind had shifted the dunes since morning. He did not look back often, but when he did, it was not to check whether she had followed.

It was to check whether she was all right.

That mattered.

Elara hated that it mattered.

"You are quiet," he said.

His voice carried easily in the open air.

She looked toward him.

"So are you."

"That is not unusual."

"No," she said. "I'm starting to understand that."

He turned slightly, and for a moment the last light caught his face, sharpening the line of his cheekbone, darkening his eyes until they seemed almost black.

"You understand very little," he said.

She should have been irritated.

Instead, she smiled faintly.

"You enjoy saying that to me."

"I do not enjoy it."

"But you keep saying it."

"Because it remains true."

She let out a soft breath, almost a laugh, but the sound disappeared quickly into the wind.

They walked a little farther.

Ahead, the sand dipped into a shallow hollow partially shielded by low scrub and a cluster of thorny bushes. A few camels stood there, quieter than the others she had seen that day. No colorful harnesses. No bells. No painted markings. Their ropes were dark and plain, their bodies lean beneath their coats, their eyes steady and alert.

Elara slowed.

The stillness around them was different from rest.

It felt trained.

Contained.

Arjun stopped at the edge of the hollow.

"Do not take pictures here," he said.

The instruction was quiet.

Absolute.

Elara's hand had not moved toward her camera, but she felt the weight of the warning anyway.

"I won't."

He looked at her for a moment, as if deciding whether to believe her.

Then he nodded once.

They stood in silence.

One of the camels turned its head toward them. Its eyes held the strange, deep calm Elara had begun to associate with the animals, but there was something else there too. Intelligence, perhaps. Or memory. The animal did not move toward them. It only watched.

A man emerged from the far side of the hollow.

Older.

Thin.

Wrapped in a pale turban that had darkened with dust at the edges. His beard was short and white, his face deeply lined, his eyes sharp in a way that made Elara straighten without meaning to.

He looked first at Arjun.

Then at her.

The pause that followed was brief, but it altered the air.

He said something in Hindi, his voice low.

Arjun answered in the same language.

Elara could not understand the words, but she understood tone.

Disapproval.

Question.

Warning.

The older man looked at her again. Not rudely. Not with curiosity. With assessment. As if she were not a woman, not a photographer, not a foreigner, but a problem being measured.

She felt heat rise along her neck.

Arjun spoke again, more quietly this time.

The man's gaze did not soften.

He stepped closer to Arjun and said something else, the words clipped, controlled.

Arjun did not move.

Did not look away.

For the first time, Elara saw a different version of him. Not the man who commanded the attention of the fair. Not the man who others moved around instinctively. Here, with this elder, his power shifted. It did not vanish, but it was held within something older. Something inherited. Something he could not simply step outside of.

The older man looked at Elara once more, then turned and walked back toward the camels.

The dismissal was complete.

Only when he had moved out of earshot did Elara speak.

"He doesn't want me here."

"No."

The answer came too quickly to soften.

She nodded, swallowing.

"And you brought me anyway."

Arjun did not look at her.

"Yes."

"Why?"

He was silent for a moment.

The wind moved lightly through the hollow, lifting dust in small threads along the ground. One of the camels lowered its head, then raised it again, slow and deliberate.

"Because you asked to see," he said finally.

"That's not the same as agreeing to show me."

"No."

She waited.

He turned toward her then.

"But you would have kept trying."

She held his gaze.

"That makes me sound foolish."

"It makes you honest."

The words struck her gently, more gently than she expected.

She looked away first.

The desert beyond the hollow was almost blue now in the failing light. The first hint of evening had settled across everything, softening the world without making it safer.

"What did he say?" she asked.

Arjun looked back toward the elder.

"He asked why you are here."

"And what did you say?"

"That you are leaving soon."

The words landed harder than she expected.

Leaving soon.

Of course she was.

She had an assignment. A return flight. A life in New York, even if she did not yet know what shape that life would take when she returned to it.

Still, hearing him say it felt like a door closing.

"And then?" she asked.

Arjun's jaw tightened slightly.

"He said that is why you should not be here."

Elara let the silence hold that for a moment.

Because she understood.

Maybe not fully.

But enough.

The danger was not only what she might see.

It was what might begin before she left.

She looked toward the camels again.

"What happens to them?"

Arjun followed her gaze.

"When?"

"At night."

His expression changed.

Only slightly.

But she saw it.

He had shown her something. But not everything. Not yet.

"Some rest," he said.

"And the others?"

A long pause.

"Elara."

Her name in his mouth carried warning.

She turned to him.

"You brought me here."

"I brought you this far."

"And now?"

"Now you decide if you need more."

The answer unsettled her because it gave the choice back to her.

She looked out over the hollow.

The older man had moved to one of the camels and was checking the rope near its head. Another man had appeared beyond him, younger, darker, his movements quick and silent. He carried something wrapped in cloth against his side.

Elara noticed because photographers notice.

Not because she meant to.

A shape.

A weight.

The way the man held it close but tried to make it look ordinary.

Her breath slowed.

The younger man knelt beside a camel. The elder shifted his body slightly, blocking part of the view.

Not enough.

Elara saw the cloth opened briefly.

Saw a smaller package inside.

Then another.

Tightly bound.

Pale.

Unmarked.

Her mouth went dry.

She knew immediately that she should look away.

She did not.

The younger man moved quickly, fastening the wrapped bundle beneath a layer of coarse fabric near the camel's side, so close to the body that from a distance it would disappear into shadow.

Arjun stepped in front of her.

Not abruptly.

But firmly.

The line of sight vanished.

"Elara."

This time her name was sharper.

She looked up at him.

The air between them had changed completely.

The softness of the afternoon was gone.

The intimacy.

The almost tenderness.

What remained was something harder.

Real.

"You saw enough," he said.

She could hear her own heartbeat now.

"I saw what they were doing."

"Yes."

The honesty shocked her.

He did not deny it.

Did not soften it.

Did not say she had misunderstood.

"What was it?" she asked, though she already knew he would not answer plainly.

He looked past her toward the direction of the fair.

"You should go back."

"No."

His eyes returned to hers.

"Elara."

"No," she repeated, quieter this time. "You don't get to show me half a truth and then tell me to walk away from the rest of it."

His expression tightened.

"This is not a story you can finish."

There it was again.

Story.

As if he understood that word could cut deeper than warning.

She took a breath, tasting dust on her tongue.

"Why are you part of this?"

He looked away.

For the first time, he looked away before answering.

The movement was small, but it told her more than words.

"I told you," he said. "Some things are inherited."

"That isn't an answer."

"It is the only one I have."

"No," she said. "It's the one you use when you don't want to give the real one."

His gaze returned to hers.

Something flared there.

Not anger alone.

Pain.

Contained so quickly she almost doubted she had seen it.

Almost.

"You believe there is a clean life and an unclean one," he said. "You come from a place where choices have names. Good. Bad. Right. Wrong."

"That's not fair."

"No," he said, his voice lowering. "It is not. But you think it anyway."

She wanted to deny it.

She couldn't.

Not entirely.

Because some part of her had been thinking exactly that. Not consciously. Not cruelly. But there, beneath her curiosity, beneath attraction and fascination, was the privilege of believing she could examine danger without being born into it.

She swallowed.

"I'm trying to understand."

"And what will that change?"

The question was quiet.

Devastatingly so.

Elara had no answer.

Behind him, one of the camels let out a low groan, the sound rolling through the hollow like something ancient. The elder looked toward them again.

Arjun noticed.

"We leave now."

This time, she did not argue.

They walked back in silence.

The fair grew louder as they approached, but not immediately. The sound returned slowly, in fragments. First voices. Then bells. Then the creak of cart wheels. Then the smell of food, thick and human and comforting in a way that felt almost jarring after what she had seen.

Elara felt dust along her skin.

In her hair.

On her lips.

She could taste it.

She could still see the wrapped bundles.

The way the elder had stepped in front.

The way Arjun had stepped in front of her.

Protection and concealment.

She was no longer sure where one ended and the other began.

At the edge of the fair, Arjun stopped.

She stopped beside him.

For a moment, neither spoke.

The fading light had turned everything copper. The world looked beautiful again, almost impossibly so. Men moved through dust and gold. Camels stood against the horizon. A child laughed somewhere nearby. The scent of frying dough drifted through the air, sweet and warm.

It was all still beautiful.

That was the cruelest part.

The beauty had not disappeared because she had seen what lived beneath it.

It had only become more complicated.

Arjun turned toward her.

"You cannot photograph this."

"I know."

"You cannot write it."

She looked at him then.

"That's not your decision."

"It is if it puts people in danger."

"People," she said softly. "Or you?"

His face changed.

Barely.

But enough.

She had found the edge of something.

He stepped closer.

Not in anger.

Not exactly.

But the space between them tightened.

"You think you know where danger begins," he said. "You do not."

Her voice was quieter now.

"Then tell me."

A pause.

The fair moved around them.

Neither moved with it.

"If you tell this story the wrong way," he said, "the men you saw will not come for the magazine. They will not come for your editor. They will not come for your city."

He leaned closer, his voice low enough that only she could hear.

"They will come here."

Elara felt the words move through her.

Here.

To him.

To Ravi.

To the elder.

To the men and animals and lives she had only begun to understand.

The assignment suddenly felt small.

Not meaningless.

But small.

A version of truth she could take back, print, polish, frame.

And there was another truth here.

One that could not be carried so easily.

"I don't want to hurt anyone," she said.

"I believe you."

The answer came quickly.

Too quickly for doubt.

It softened something in her.

"Then why do you look at me like you don't?"

His eyes held hers.

"Because wanting does not make you safe."

The words struck her in a place she was not expecting.

Wanting does not make you safe.

She had learned that before.

With Luca.

In New York.

In rooms where desire had disguised itself as intimacy. In mornings where she had mistaken longing for proof.

She looked away, just briefly.

Arjun noticed.

Of course he did.

"What did I say?" he asked.

She shook her head.

"Nothing."

"Elara."

She looked back at him.

The softness in his voice made it harder to hide.

"Someone once made me believe wanting was enough," she said.

The admission left her before she could reconsider it.

The desert seemed to quiet around them.

Arjun did not speak.

He only watched her.

Not with pity.

Not with triumph.

With stillness.

The kind that made it possible to say more.

"I thought if I wanted something badly enough, if I stayed long enough, if I understood him enough, it would become something real."

Her voice was steady, though she felt the vulnerability of it in every word.

"It didn't."

Arjun's gaze moved over her face, slowly, carefully.

"And still you came here," he said.

It wasn't judgment.

It was recognition.

Elara let out a soft breath.

"Yes."

A silence settled between them.

Different from the others.

Quieter.

More intimate.

He looked as if he might say something.

Then didn't.

Instead, he turned toward the fair, toward the lanterns being lit one by one as the day gave itself over to night.

"You should eat," he said.

The shift was so unexpected that she almost laughed.

"I should eat?"

"Yes."

"That's what you have to say?"

"You have not eaten since morning."

She stared at him.

"How could you possibly know that?"

He did not look at her.

"You carry yourself differently when you are hungry."

A small, startled smile escaped her.

For a moment, the heaviness loosened.

Only a little.

But enough.

"And you noticed that?"

He glanced at her then.

"I notice many things."

The smile faded slowly, but not because she was unhappy.

Because the words landed somewhere deeper.

He did.

He noticed things.

The dangerous things.

The small things.

Her movements.

Her silence.

The way she looked at the world.

The way she tried not to look at him.

He began walking again, this time toward the food stalls near the outer edge of the fair.

After a moment, she followed.

They stopped at a small stall where a man was pressing dough between his palms before laying it onto a hot surface. Steam rose immediately. Oil hissed. The air filled with warmth and spice.

Arjun spoke to the man, who nodded and began preparing two plates.

Elara stood beside him, still unsettled by what she had seen, still aware of the danger, but now surrounded by the ordinary intimacy of food being made by hand.

The first bite was hot enough to burn her fingers.

She tore off a piece carefully, dipping it into a thick sauce that smelled of tomatoes, cumin, and chili. The flavor burst across her tongue.

Warm.

Sharp.

Deeply spiced.

Alive.

She closed her eyes without meaning to.

When she opened them, Arjun was watching her.

"What?" she asked.

"You look surprised every time the food has flavor."

She laughed then.

A real laugh.

Soft, but real.

"Because it does. Every time."

He looked away, but she saw the corner of his mouth shift.

Almost a smile.

Almost.

They ate standing side by side, their shoulders not touching, though she was aware of the space between them with almost painful clarity.

Around them, the fair began its evening transformation. Lanterns glowed. Fires were lit. Shadows lengthened and multiplied. The camels became shapes instead of animals, silhouettes against a darkening sky. The desert cooled slowly, the air brushing over her skin with a softness that felt almost impossible after the heat of the day.

And beneath it all, what she had seen remained.

The hollow.

The elder.

The packages.

The way Arjun had stood between her and the truth.

She looked at him.

"You knew I would see something."

He did not deny it.

"Yes."

"Then why take me?"

He finished the bite in his hand before answering.

"Because if I kept telling you to leave, you would only imagine worse."

"And this is better?"

"No."

He turned toward her.

"But now you know enough to be careful."

She studied him.

"Is that what this is? You trying to make me careful?"

His gaze held hers.

"Yes."

The honesty moved through her slowly.

Not romantic.

Not soft.

Something deeper than either.

A man like Luca had never tried to make her careful. He had wanted her reckless because it served him. He had wanted her available, wanting, waiting, willing to be pulled into whatever storm he created.

Arjun was different.

Not safe.

Never safe.

But different.

He was danger that understood danger.

That was worse, perhaps.

Or better.

She did not yet know.

They finished eating as the night thickened around them.

When she handed her empty plate back to the stall owner, her fingers brushed Arjun's briefly. It was nothing. An accident, easily dismissed.

Neither of them dismissed it.

For a moment, they stood too still.

Then Arjun stepped back.

Not far.

Just enough.

"You go back now," he said.

This time, she did not argue.

The day had given her too much.

The desert had given her too much.

He walked her to the edge of the camp, but no farther. The red carpets glowed under lantern light, their patterns dark and rich against the sand. Beyond them, the tents stood in quiet rows, soft and temporary beneath the vastness of the sky.

Elara stopped before stepping onto the carpet.

She turned to him.

"What happens now?"

The question surprised her.

She had meant the story.

The assignment.

The secret.

But as soon as she said it, she knew it meant more.

Arjun looked at her for a long moment.

"Now," he said quietly, "you decide what kind of truth you can carry."

The words settled into her.

Heavy.

Beautiful.

Terrifying.

She stepped onto the carpet.

Then turned back once.

He was still there.

Of course he was.

The desert behind him had gone dark, but she could see him clearly enough. His shape. His stillness. The line between where he stood and where she belonged.

For the first time, the distance between them felt visible.

Not wide.

Not impossible.

But real.

And as Elara walked back toward her tent, dust still on her skin, spice still warm on her tongue, she understood that she had crossed into something she could no longer pretend was only fascination.

She had seen what the desert hid.

And now the desert had seen something in her too.

CHAPTER EIGHTEEN

The Baddest Boy of All

She did not sleep well.

The desert followed her into the tent.

Not in sound.

In feeling.

Dust remained along her arms even after she washed. Fine, pale traces gathered at the edges of her skin, beneath her fingernails, in the folds of fabric she had worn all day. The hot water had arrived at her tent door before dawn, just as they had promised it would, carried in a brass-colored vessel by a man who placed it quietly beside the entrance and disappeared without waiting to be thanked.

Elara had bathed in silence.

Still, she could not wash the day away.

The hollow.

The elder's eyes.

The packages wrapped in cloth.

Arjun stepping in front of her, not to shield her from danger exactly, but from seeing too much of it.

Or perhaps both.

She stood now before the small mirror inside her tent, the canvas walls glowing faintly with the last remnants of lantern light. Outside, the camp had quieted. Dinner had ended hours ago. The last murmur of voices had faded into the stillness of night.

But inside her, nothing was still.

She wrapped the cloth more tightly around her shoulders and sat on the edge of the bed.

Her camera rested on the table nearby.

She had not looked at the photographs.

Not once since returning.

That alone unsettled her.

Usually, reviewing the day's images was ritual. A way of organizing the world after moving through it. A way of deciding what mattered, what had been captured, what still needed to be found.

Tonight, she could not bring herself to look.

Because she already knew what mattered.

And it was not in the camera.

It was in what she had seen when she had not been shooting.

Elara leaned forward, elbows on her knees, and pressed her palms lightly together.

She thought of Luca.

Not because she wanted to.

Because some part of her finally had to.

He came back to her in pieces.

A dark hallway in New York.

The smell of expensive cologne and cigarette smoke clinging to his shirt.

A hand around her wrist, not hard, but possessive enough to make her mistake it for desire.

His laugh when she asked where he had been.

His silence when she needed him to answer.

He had been beautiful in the way a fast car was beautiful before the crash.

Dangerous, polished, designed to make people look.

And she had looked.

She had done more than look.

She had followed.

For months, she had let herself be pulled into the rhythm of him. Late nights. Missed calls. Apologies that never fully arrived. Promises that sounded true only because she wanted them to.

Her friends had told her.

Her sister had told her.

Her own body had told her.

Still, she had stayed.

Not because she was foolish.

She knew better than that.

Because wanting had made her hopeful.

Because intensity had made her feel chosen.

Because part of her had believed that if she could love a wild thing enough, it might become gentle in her hands.

She closed her eyes.

And then she saw Arjun.

Standing in the desert at dusk.

Dark hair touched by fading light.

Stillness where Luca had been motion.

Control where Luca had been chaos.

A man built from shadow, restraint, and heat.

The thought rose before she could stop it.

This is the baddest boy of all.

Her eyes opened.

The words startled her because they were not dramatic.

They were honest.

Not Luca with his money, his drugs, his women, his beautiful recklessness, his need to be wanted by everyone and loyal to no one.

Arjun was something else.

Deeper.

Darker.

More dangerous because he did not pretend otherwise.

Luca had been a boy playing at ruin.

Arjun was a man who lived inside it.

And still, she wanted to understand him.

Still, she wanted to be near him.

Still, some reckless part of her looked at the danger and felt not repelled, but drawn closer.

Elara stood abruptly, as if movement could interrupt the thought.

It didn't.

She crossed the tent and poured a small amount of water into a cup. The water tasted faintly metallic, warmed by the room, but she drank it anyway.

What are you doing?

The question had followed her since New York.

It sounded like her mother.

Like her friends.

Like the voice she used on herself when she was tired of defending choices she could not fully explain.

What are you doing?

She looked toward the camera.

Toward the notebook beside it.

Her assignment notes were there. Neatly written. Professional. Useful.

Pushkar Camel Fair.

Livestock trade.

Nomadic communities.

Ritual, color, economy, spectacle.

All true.

All incomplete.

She moved to the table and sat. The chair creaked softly beneath her.

For several minutes, she only stared at the notebook.

Then she opened it.

The pen felt cool in her hand.

She wrote one line.

There are parts of the fair that are not meant to be photographed.

She stopped.

The words looked back at her.

Not dramatic.

Not enough.

She continued.

There are men here who move as if the desert belongs to them. Or as if they belong to it so completely that the difference no longer matters.

She paused again.

Then, beneath it, without meaning to, she wrote his name.

Arjun Rathore.

She stared at it.

The ink seemed too dark on the page.

Too permanent.

Outside, something moved beyond the tent. A soft step in sand. A faint shift of fabric. Then nothing.

Elara looked up.

Listened.

The silence returned.

She told herself it was one of the camp staff.

Someone checking lanterns.

Someone moving between tents.

But her body had already become alert.

The way it did when she knew she was not alone.

She stood slowly and moved toward the entrance.

For a moment, she did nothing.

Then she lifted the canvas flap.

The night was wide and cool.

Lanterns burned low along the carpeted paths, their light softened by the darkness, their glow turning the red carpets almost black in places. The tents stood in quiet rows, their shapes luminous beneath the night sky.

Beyond the camp, the desert stretched dark and open.

No one stood near her tent.

Still, she felt watched.

Not threatened.

Seen.

She stepped outside.

The air touched her face, cooler now, carrying a faint trace of smoke from distant fires. Somewhere far beyond the camp, a camel groaned low in the night. The sound rolled across the sand, strange and lonely.

Elara looked toward the fair.

Most of it was hidden now.

Only the occasional lantern marked its edges.

During the day, it had been color and movement. At night, it became outline and suggestion. Things half seen. Things imagined.

She should go back inside.

Instead, she remained where she was.

A few minutes later, she saw him.

Not close.

Not at the edge of her tent.

Farther out, where the last of the camp light gave way to darkness.

Arjun stood with another man near the boundary between camp and fair. The man spoke with his hands held low, his body angled away. Arjun listened without moving.

Even from this distance, she knew it was him.

His stillness was unmistakable.

Elara should have stepped back into the tent before he saw her.

She didn't.

The other man turned and left, disappearing into the dark beyond the lanterns.

Arjun remained.

Then his head lifted.

Their eyes met across the distance.

Of course.

Something passed through her.

Not surprise.

Not fear.

Recognition.

For a long moment, neither moved.

Then he began walking toward her.

Slowly.

Not as if summoned.

Not as if caught.

As if he had already known this would happen.

Elara let the tent flap fall behind her.

She stood barefoot now at the edge of the carpet, the sand cool where it touched her heels.

Arjun stopped a few feet away.

Too close for indifference.

Not close enough for touch.

"You are awake," he said.

"So are you."

"This is not unusual."

She almost smiled.

"You've said that before."

"Because it remains true."

The faint echo of their earlier conversation settled between them, but neither laughed.

The night did not allow for it.

"What were you doing out there?" she asked.

His gaze moved briefly past her, toward the tents, then returned.

"Work."

"At this hour?"

"Especially at this hour."

The answer carried enough truth to end the question.

It did not end hers.

"What kind of work?"

"Elara."

Her name again.

Warning and invitation together.

She looked at him in the lantern light.

He was different at night.

Not softer.

More dangerous, maybe, because less of him was visible. The shadows gathered along his face, darkened the hollow beneath his cheekbones, deepened his eyes until they looked almost unreadable.

Almost.

"You told me I need to decide what kind of truth I can carry," she said.

"Yes."

"How can I decide that if you keep deciding what I'm allowed to know?"

His expression did not change immediately.

But she saw something move beneath it.

"You think knowledge is freedom," he said.

"Isn't it?"

"No."

The answer was immediate.

"Sometimes it is a chain."

The words settled into the cool air.

Elara looked past him toward the dark.

"Is that what this is for you?"

A pause.

Longer this time.

"Yes."

The honesty of it struck her.

She had expected deflection. He gave her truth instead.

At least part of it.

"Then why don't you leave?" she asked.

The question was too simple.

She knew that as soon as she said it.

Arjun's gaze sharpened, but not with anger.

With something older.

"Because leaving is not the same for everyone."

Elara felt the quiet rebuke.

She deserved it.

"I know," she said.

"No," he replied. "You do not."

The words should have pushed her back.

Instead, they humbled her.

She looked down for a moment, at the edge of the carpet beneath her feet. Red thread. Gold pattern. Sand already creeping over the border, softening its precision.

"You're right," she said.

The admission surprised him.

She could see that.

Only slightly.

But enough.

"I don't know," she continued. "But I want to."

The silence that followed felt different.

Not argument.

Not distance.

Something opening.

A camel called again in the dark, farther away this time.

Arjun looked toward the sound.

When he spoke, his voice was lower.

"My father died when I was young."

Elara stilled.

She had not expected that.

He did not look at her as he said it.

"He knew the desert better than any man I have ever known. He knew where water would be before the ground showed it. He knew when an animal would fail before it did. He knew which men could be trusted and which ones would sell their own blood if the price was high enough."

His gaze stayed on the darkness.

"When he died, many people came to our house. Men who had worked with him. Men who owed him. Men he owed. They spoke to my mother as if grief were something that could be negotiated."

Elara said nothing.

She barely breathed.

"I was not old enough to decide anything," he said. "But I was old enough for them to decide for me."

The words entered her slowly.

Not like confession.

Like history.

Something carved into him before he had a chance to choose.

"This work," she said quietly.

He looked back at her.

"This life," he corrected.

The distinction mattered.

She felt it immediately.

"I'm sorry," she said.

He shook his head once.

"Do not be sorry for what you do not understand."

It was not cruel.

Only precise.

Elara nodded.

They stood in silence again.

The lantern between them flickered, light shifting across his face, then hers.

She could see him more clearly now.

Not the man she had first noticed beside the lean camel.

Not the mysterious auctioneer who moved through danger with impossible calm.

A boy once.

A son.

Someone shaped.

Someone claimed.

And still, the thought returned.

This is the baddest boy of all.

Only now the words carried a different ache.

Not fantasy.

Not thrill.

Recognition.

The baddest boy of all because he was not pretending to be broken. He was not performing danger to make himself more desirable. He had been built inside something dark and had learned how to survive there.

That made him more dangerous.

And more human.

Elara felt the old pattern flare inside her.

The pull toward the man she could not save.

The urge to find the wound and press herself against it, as if love could close what life had opened.

She almost stepped back.

Not from him.

From herself.

Arjun noticed.

"What is it?"

She let out a soft breath.

"I'm trying to decide if I'm seeing you clearly."

"And?"

"I don't know yet."

His gaze held hers.

"At least that is honest."

She laughed softly, but there was no humor in it.

"I'm not sure honesty is helping me."

"It rarely does at first."

That almost made her smile.

Almost.

He looked at her then in a way that felt less guarded than before.

"You are thinking of someone."

The accuracy of it unsettled her.

She looked away.

"Yes."

"The man you left."

The words were not a question.

Elara's throat tightened.

"He wasn't someone I left," she said. "Not exactly."

Arjun waited.

"He was someone I kept returning to," she said.

The admission came slowly.

"He was beautiful. Reckless. Unfaithful. Untouchable in the way people mistake for power."

Arjun's face did not change, but his attention sharpened.

"I thought wanting him meant something," she continued. "I thought if I could make him choose me, then it would prove something about me."

The night seemed to hold the words.

"And did it?" he asked.

"No."

She looked back at him.

"It proved the opposite."

For a moment, she wished she had not said that.

It was too much.

Too revealing.

But Arjun did not move closer.

He did not reach for her.

He did not use the vulnerability.

That alone made something inside her ache.

"What did it prove?" he asked.

She swallowed.

"That I didn't know the difference between being wanted and being loved."

The truth landed fully only after she said it.

Arjun was very still.

Then, quietly, he said, "Many people do not."

She looked at him.

"Including you?"

A long pause.

The lantern flickered again.

"I know the difference," he said.

Something in his voice changed.

Barely.

"But that does not mean I have lived it."

Elara felt the words move through her.

The distance between them seemed smaller now.

Not physically.

Something else.

She became aware of the night around them. The cool air along her arms. The scent of smoke in his clothes. The faint spice still lingering on her own breath from dinner. The sand beneath her bare feet.

Everything felt too close.

Too clear.

"Arjun," she said.

His name came out softer than she intended.

He heard it.

She knew he did.

For a moment, neither spoke.

Then he looked away.

Not abruptly.

Deliberately.

Control returning.

"You should go inside."

She almost laughed.

Not because it was funny.

Because of course.

Of course that was where he would go.

Distance.

Restraint.

The line drawn again.

"And you?" she asked.

"I go back."

"To the fair?"

"Yes."

"At this hour?"

He looked at her.

"Especially at this hour."

They stood there a moment longer.

Then Elara nodded.

This time, she did not argue.

She turned toward her tent, lifted the flap, then paused.

When she looked back, he was still there.

Still watching.

Still impossible.

"Arjun?"

"Yes."

"What if I don't want you to go back?"

The question changed the air.

She knew it immediately.

His face remained still, but something in him went taut.

"Elara."

"I know," she said softly. "I know."

But she didn't take it back.

A long silence passed between them.

Then he said, "Wanting does not make a thing possible."

The words should have closed the moment.

Instead, they broke something open.

Because they both knew now.

This was not only her wanting.

He turned before she could answer.

Not quickly.

Not dramatically.

But with the discipline of a man who understood exactly what staying would cost.

Elara watched him walk back toward the darkness beyond the camp, his figure narrowing into shadow until the desert took him.

Only then did she step inside.

She sat on the edge of the bed for a long time after that, the tent around her warm and dim, the night outside alive with things she could no longer pretend not to hear.

At last, she reached for her notebook.

Her hand moved before she knew what she meant to write.

The baddest boys do not always arrive loud. Sometimes they stand very still and tell the truth.

She stared at the line.

Then closed the notebook.

Outside, the desert waited.

And somewhere beyond the last lantern, so did he.

CHAPTER NINETEEN

The Line You Feel Before You Cross It

The morning came softer than she expected. After a night that had refused to settle, Elara thought the desert might wake harsh, unforgiving, as if it had something to prove. Instead, the light arrived gently, filtering through the canvas of her tent in muted gold, the edges of the world still blurred by sleep and shadow. For a moment, she lay still, not fully awake, not fully resting, suspended. She remembered everything. Not in pieces. In full. Arjun standing at the edge of the dark. The way he had said her name. The story of his father. The way he had turned away when she asked him to stay. And beneath all of it, the feeling.

Elara closed her eyes again, pressing her hand lightly against her chest as if she could quiet something that had already moved beyond her control. You are choosing this. The thought came clearly. Not as judgment.

As truth. She sat up slowly, the fabric of the bed shifting beneath her, the air inside the tent already warming with the rising sun. The world outside had begun again. Soft footsteps. Muted voices. The quiet rhythm of morning preparations. She could stay. For the first time since arriving, she could choose to stay within the safe edges of the camp. Drink tea. Review her photographs. Write her notes. Complete the assignment the way it was meant to be completed. She could leave this place with a story. And leave everything else behind. The thought lasted only a moment. Then it dissolved.

Elara stood. She dressed with less hesitation now, her movements grounded, deliberate. The cloth wrapped around her waist settled into place more easily. The mirror reflected someone she almost recognized. Not entirely. But closer. When she stepped outside, the air met her with a faint warmth, carrying the scent of chai already brewing somewhere nearby. Cardamom. Milk. Steam rising into the cool morning. She took a cup without speaking, nodding to the man who handed it to her. The first sip anchored her immediately. Sweet. Spiced. Familiar now. Everything here was becoming familiar. That should have been comforting. Instead, it made everything more complicated.

Elara moved through the early fair with her camera, capturing the quiet moments that most people overlooked. A man washing his hands in a small basin, water spilling into the sand below. A camel still kneeling, not yet called into motion, its eyes half-lidded, its breath slow and steady. She worked like that for a while. Grounded. Present. But she felt it. Of course she did. The awareness didn't arrive anymore. It lived inside her. She turned. He wasn't there. For a moment, something in her stilled. Not disappointment. Not relief. Something in between. She lowered the camera slowly. Good. The word formed in her mind before she could stop it. Good.

Because if he wasn't there, she could finish her work. She could stay within the story she had come to tell. She could remain in control of something that had begun to feel dangerously uncontained.

She lifted the camera again. A trader adjusting his scarf, the fabric catching the light. A group of women laughing quietly, their hands moving as they spoke. She moved forward. Focused. Intentional. And still, something pulled. Not from outside. From within. Elara lowered the camera again. This isn't about him. She told herself that. It didn't hold. She turned once more. And this time, he was there. Closer than before. Not watching from a distance. Not waiting at the edge. Standing within her space. As if he had always been there. As if the moment she had tried not to look was the moment he chose to appear.

Their eyes met. And everything shifted again. Not sharply. Inevitably. Elara didn't hesitate this time. She stepped toward him. He didn't move. Not forward. Not back. Just remained. The space between them closed. Not quickly. Deliberately. "You weren't here," she said. Her voice was softer than she expected. "I was." A pause. "You didn't see me." The words carried something subtle. Not accusation. Not challenge. Observation. Elara felt it. "I was working," she said. "I know." Silence settled between them. But it wasn't empty. It was full of everything they were not saying.

Elara shifted slightly, the sand pressing beneath her feet. "I thought about what you said," she said. "Which part?" "All of it." A faint shift moved through his expression. "And?" he asked. She held his gaze. "I'm still here." The answer was simple. Honest. Arjun exhaled slowly. "Yes." There was no resistance in it now. Only recognition. Elara stepped closer. This time, closer than before. The air between them changed. Warmer. More present. "You didn't answer me last night," she said. A pause. "I asked you not to go back." His gaze sharpened slightly. "And you asked me to stay," he said. The words landed. Neither of them looked away.

Elara felt her pulse shift. "I didn't mean it the way it sounded," she said. A small lie. He heard it. "Yes, you did." The honesty of it pulled something loose inside her. She let out a breath. "I don't know what I meant." That part was true. Silence stretched. The fair moved around them. Voices rising. Camels shifting. Life continuing. But the space between them felt separate from all of it. "You are trying to understand something that does not have a clean answer," he said. His voice was lower now. Closer. "I know," she said. "Then why continue?" The question settled heavily.

Elara didn't answer immediately. Because she didn't have a clean answer. Because the truth wasn't simple. Finally, "Because I don't want to walk away from it," she said. The words came quiet. But they held. Arjun's gaze held hers. For a moment, something shifted. Not outwardly. Beneath. "You should," he said. The words were softer now. Almost reluctant. Elara shook her head slightly. "I know." A pause. "But I won't." There it was. The choice. Clear. Unavoidable.

The air between them felt different now. Not just charged. Fragile. As if something had moved too close to the surface. Arjun stepped closer. This time, fully closing the space between them. Not touching. But close enough that Elara could feel the heat of him. The scent of him. Smoke. Sand. Something darker beneath it. Her breath shifted. "You are standing at a line," he said. His voice was barely above the air between them. "And you feel it." Elara didn't move. "Yes." A pause. "And you know you should not cross it." Another truth. "Yes."

Silence. The world seemed to narrow. The sounds of the fair faded. The light sharpened. Everything reduced to the space between them. And still, neither moved. Neither stepped back. Elara became aware of everything. The warmth of the air. The texture of the sand beneath her feet. The faint movement of his breath. The way her body leaned, almost imperceptibly, toward him. And then he reached out. Slowly. Deliberately. His hand lifted. Not to pull her in. Not to claim. But to hover just at the edge of her arm. As if asking a question.

Elara felt it before he touched her. The line. The moment. The choice. And for one second, she almost crossed it. Then Arjun pulled his hand back. The space returned. Sharp. Immediate. Elara's breath caught. "What are you doing?" she whispered. The question wasn't accusation. It was something else. He held her gaze. "Not crossing it." The words landed with quiet force.

Elara felt something inside her shift. Not disappointment. Something deeper. Understanding. Because he had stopped them. Not because he didn't want to. Because he did. The realization moved through her slowly. And that made it more dangerous. They stood there for a moment longer. Then, without another word, Arjun stepped back. The distance returned. This time, it felt different. Not like protection. Like restraint.

CHAPTER TWENTY

The Men Who Watch

By afternoon, the fair felt different.

Elara noticed it before she could name it.

The movement was still there. Camels shifted and groaned under the sun. Traders gathered in clusters, their voices rising and falling in practiced rhythm. Children darted between animals and carts with the same careless confidence they had carried since she arrived.

The colors remained.

The dust remained.

The heat remained.

And yet, something had changed.

Not in the fair itself.

In the way it received her.

She felt it as she moved through the crowd with her camera against her chest. The glances came more often now. Short. Controlled. Not curious in the way they had been before.

Measured.

Remembering.

She had been seen too many times in the wrong places.

And more dangerously…

she had been seen with him.

Elara lifted her camera, but her hands were less steady than usual.

Click.

A camel kneeling in the sand.

Click.

A trader tying a rope around his wrist while speaking to another man.

Click.

A child watching her from behind his father's leg.

She lowered the camera.

The child did not smile.

Neither did the father.

A breeze moved through the fair, lifting dust into the air. It brushed across her lips, gritty and dry. She tasted sand and spice and something metallic beneath it, as if the desert itself were warning her.

She turned slightly.

Arjun was nowhere in sight.

That should have eased something.

It didn't.

A voice spoke behind her.

"Miss Quinn."

She turned quickly.

Ravi stood a few feet away, his expression more serious than she had seen it before.

"Ravi," she said, trying to soften her own face into something normal. "I didn't see you."

"No," he said. "You were not looking."

There was no judgment in the words.

But there was meaning.

Elara adjusted the strap of her camera.

"Is something wrong?"

Ravi looked past her, toward the quieter edge of the fair.

Then back.

"You should come back to camp."

The words landed with quiet force.

"Why?"

He hesitated.

That was answer enough.

"Ravi."

His gaze lowered for a moment, then lifted again.

"Some men are asking questions."

A slow chill moved through her despite the afternoon heat.

"What kind of questions?"

"About you."

She looked toward the crowd around them, suddenly aware of every face, every pause, every man who turned away just before she could meet his eyes.

"What are they asking?"

"Why you come here. Why you return to places where visitors do not go. Why Arjun speaks with you."

There it was.

The truth spoken plainly.

Elara's fingers tightened around the camera.

"What did you say?"

Ravi's expression softened slightly, but only slightly.

"That you are here for photographs. For magazine. That you leave soon."

Leaving soon.

Again those words.

They were becoming a kind of shield. A reason others should tolerate her presence. A promise that whatever disruption she caused would be temporary.

She looked away.

"And did they believe you?"

Ravi did not answer quickly enough.

"Some things do not need belief," he said. "Only patience."

"What does that mean?"

"It means they wait for you to leave."

The words should have comforted her.

They did not.

Because she heard the warning beneath them.

They were patient because she was temporary.

But if she became something more than temporary, patience could end.

Ravi stepped closer, lowering his voice.

"You are kind woman. I know this. But here, kindness does not protect you from mistake."

Elara felt the weight of that.

"I'm not trying to make trouble."

"I know."

He looked toward the quiet edge of the fair again.

"That is not always enough."

She followed his gaze.

The far section seemed still from this distance, almost empty beneath the hard afternoon light. But now she knew better. Nothing there was empty. Nothing there was still.

"Did Arjun send you?" she asked.

Ravi's face changed.

Just enough.

"No."

The answer came too quickly.

Elara stared at him.

"He did."

Ravi's jaw tightened.

"He said if I saw you alone, I should bring you back."

The words struck her in a place she was not prepared for.

Concern.

Control.

Protection.

All of it tangled together until she could not tell which one she resented and which one she wanted.

"I don't need to be brought back like a child."

Ravi's expression remained steady.

"No," he said. "But you need to be alive to be angry about it."

The words were so blunt that for a moment she had no answer.

Around them, the fair continued. A camel groaned low nearby. Someone laughed in the distance. Oil hissed in a pan, sending up the smell of fried dough and chili.

Life did not pause for her realization.

Ravi held out a hand, not touching her, only gesturing.

"Come."

Elara did not move.

Not at first.

She looked once more toward the far edge of the fair.

A man stood there now.

Older.

Thin.

A pale turban wrapped around his head.

The elder from the hollow.

He was watching her.

Not openly.

Not dramatically.

Simply standing.

Seeing.

Elara's breath slowed.

Then, very deliberately, she turned back toward the camp.

Ravi walked beside her.

Neither of them spoke.

The red carpets appeared ahead, impossibly elegant against the sand. The transition back into camp felt almost absurd now. Polished trays. Brass cups. Folded linens. Soft voices. Vegetarian dishes fragrant with cumin, lentils, ginger, and warm ghee.

A world built for comfort.

Just steps away from one built on secrets.

Elara stopped outside her tent.

"Thank you," she said.

Ravi nodded.

Then he hesitated.

"Miss Quinn."

"Yes?"

He looked at her carefully.

"Some stories are heavy. You do not know this until you carry them."

The words stayed with her after he left.

Inside the tent, the air felt too still.

Elara set her camera down on the table and stared at it.

For the first time since arriving, the object looked different to her.

Not like a tool.

Like evidence.

She sat and opened her notebook.

The pages were filled now with observations, fragments, names, sensory notes, pieces of dialogue, descriptions of color and movement and trade.

But the truth of the fair had grown beyond what she could safely write.

She picked up her pen.

The tip hovered over the page.

Then she wrote:

A story can become dangerous when it belongs to people who cannot leave it.

She stared at the sentence.

Then another came.

What right do I have to carry home what others must survive?

Her throat tightened.

That was the question.

Not whether the story mattered.

It did.

Not whether the hidden world existed.

It did.

But what right did she have to take it?

A sound outside made her lift her head.

Footsteps.

Not soft.

Not hesitant.

She knew before the shadow crossed the tent opening.

"Come in," she said.

The flap lifted.

Arjun stepped inside.

The tent felt smaller immediately.

He had never been inside her tent before.

The awareness of that moved through her quickly, sharply, before she could stop it. He stood just inside the entrance, bringing with him the heat of the afternoon, the scent of sand and smoke, the energy of the world beyond the carpets.

His gaze moved first to her face.

Then to the notebook.

Then to the camera on the table.

"You came back," she said.

"I heard Ravi found you."

"Did he report to you?"

The edge in her voice was impossible to miss.

Arjun's expression did not change.

"No."

"But you asked him to watch me."

"Yes."

The honesty irritated her more than denial would have.

"You don't get to do that."

"I know."

"And yet you did."

"Yes."

She stood.

The movement brought them closer, though several feet still separated them.

"You can't decide where I go."

"No."

"You can't decide what I photograph."

"No."

"You can't decide what I write."

His eyes held hers.

"No," he said. "But I can tell you what it may cost."

The words quieted something in her.

Not fully.

But enough.

Arjun looked toward the notebook again.

"What did you write?"

"That's mine."

"Yes."

His gaze returned to hers.

"And some of what you have written is not."

The sentence landed hard.

Elara felt it like a hand on her chest.

Not because it was cruel.

Because it was true.

She looked away first.

Outside, someone passed along the carpeted path, footsteps softened by woven fabric. A faint scent of coriander drifted in with the air.

"You think I'm using this," she said.

"I think you do not know yet what this is."

"And you do?"

"Yes."

The certainty returned.

It angered her because part of her trusted it.

"Then tell me."

He took a breath.

"Elara."

"No," she said. "Don't say my name like that. Don't warn me and then disappear into half answers. Don't bring me close and then tell everyone else to keep me away."

His face tightened.

"You think this is closeness?"

The question struck her.

"Yes," she said.

The word came before she could protect herself from it.

Silence filled the tent.

The air seemed to still between them.

Arjun did not move.

Neither did she.

Outside, the fair continued somewhere beyond the camp, muffled now, as if the canvas walls had turned the world into memory.

"You should not say things like that," he said quietly.

"Why?"

"Because words become things here."

The answer softened her anger.

Only slightly.

"What does that mean?"

"It means people hear what is not spoken."

She thought of the elder.

The men watching.

Ravi's warning.

"And they've heard us," she said.

"They have seen enough."

Her breath caught.

There it was.

Not imagined.

Not exaggerated.

Enough.

"What happens now?" she asked.

He looked at her for a long moment.

"Nothing, if you are careful."

"And if I'm not?"

His silence was worse than any answer.

Elara crossed her arms lightly, not in defense, but because she needed to hold herself still.

"Are you in danger because of me?"

He did not answer.

"Arjun."

His name changed the space just as hers did when he said it.

Finally, he said, "Not yet."

Not yet.

The words chilled her.

She sat slowly on the edge of the bed.

For the first time, the consequences of their connection moved beyond romance, beyond attraction, beyond private longing.

They could cost him something.

They could cost others something.

And she was not sure she knew how to stop what had already begun.

Arjun remained standing.

The distance between them felt larger now than it had before.

"I didn't mean for this to happen," she said.

"I know."

"I didn't come here for you."

"I know."

She looked at him then.

"But now you're here."

The truth lay between them.

No metaphor.

No evasion.

He looked away for a moment, and in that brief movement she saw the strain in him.

The control.

The effort.

When he looked back, his voice was lower.

"I am always here."

The words were not romantic.

They were harder than that.

Rooted.

Bound.

He was not a man passing through his own life. He was part of the place. Claimed by it. Watched by it. Judged by it.

And she was the woman who would leave.

The knowledge pressed against her ribs.

"I don't know what to do," she said.

It was the most honest thing she had said all day.

Arjun looked at her.

"For today," he said, "do nothing."

She almost laughed.

"That's your advice?"

"Yes."

"That sounds impossible."

"For you, maybe."

This time, a small smile almost came.

Almost.

But it faded quickly.

He stepped toward the table and looked down at the camera.

"May I see?"

The question surprised her.

"See what?"

"What you photographed today."

She hesitated.

Then picked up the camera and handed it to him.

Their fingers did not touch this time.

She noticed.

So did he.

Arjun looked at the screen as she showed him the images. The working camels. The traders. The food stalls. The boy watching from behind his father. The line of animals against the pale afternoon sky.

He studied each one with a seriousness that made her self-conscious.

Not because she doubted the work.

Because she cared what he saw.

"This one," he said.

She looked at the screen.

It was a photograph of an older man sitting beside a camel, his hand resting on the animal's folded leg. There was no drama in it. No spectacle. Only closeness, use, endurance.

"What about it?" she asked.

"This is true."

The simplicity moved her.

"Thank you."

He looked at the next image.

Then another.

He stopped on a photograph she had taken without realizing it would matter.

The elder in the pale turban.

Far in the background.

Barely visible.

But unmistakable to both of them.

Arjun's hand stilled.

Elara felt the air change.

"I didn't know he was in the frame," she said quickly.

Arjun did not answer.

"I can delete it."

He looked at her then.

"Yes."

No hesitation.

She took the camera back and deleted the image.

The tiny act felt larger than it should have.

A photograph gone.

A piece of evidence erased.

A choice made.

When she looked up, Arjun was watching her in a way she had not seen before.

Not relieved.

Not grateful.

Something quieter.

"You did not argue," he said.

"No."

"Why?"

She looked down at the camera in her hands.

"Because not everything I can take belongs to me."

The words settled between them.

Arjun's expression changed.

Barely.

But deeply.

For the first time, she saw the impact of her restraint.

Not curiosity.

Not desire.

Respect.

It moved through her more powerfully than if he had touched her.

Outside, the sky began to change. The afternoon light shifted warmer, leaning toward evening. The tent glowed softly around them.

He stepped back.

"You should stay in camp tonight."

She looked up.

"Will you?"

A pause.

"No."

Of course.

She nodded once.

Not fighting it.

Not this time.

He moved toward the entrance, then stopped.

Without turning fully, he said, "They will watch less if you do not look for me."

The words were practical.

Painful.

Necessary.

"And you?" she asked.

His shoulders remained still.

"Will you watch less?"

He turned then.

His eyes met hers.

"No."

The answer was quiet.

Immediate.

Devastating.

Then he left.

Elara stood in the tent long after the flap settled back into place.

The camera remained in her hands.

Her notebook lay open on the table.

Outside, the camp moved toward evening. Lanterns would be lit soon. Food would be served. The air would fill again with spice and smoke and the soft murmur of people pretending the night was gentle.

She looked down at the camera.

At the dark screen.

At her own reflection faintly visible in the glass.

There were things she had come here to capture.

And things she had already learned to let disappear.

For the first time, she understood that both could change a person.

She closed the notebook.

Then, slowly, she placed the camera beside it.

Tonight, she would not go looking for him.

But somewhere beyond the carpets, beyond the last safe light of the camp, she knew he would be there.

Watching less for her sake.

And not less at all.

CHAPTER TWENTY-ONE

The Night She Stayed

Elara stayed in camp that night.

That was what she told herself, as if obedience could be simple if she named it clearly enough.

She stayed.

She did not step beyond the last red carpet. She did not follow the pull toward the fair. She did not search for Arjun in the shadows beyond the lanterns, though every part of her seemed to know exactly where the darkness began.

And somehow, that took more strength than leaving ever had.

Dinner was served beneath a wide canvas canopy strung with low lanterns, their light soft and amber against the deepening night. Brass bowls caught the glow, each filled with something fragrant and warm — lentils thick with spice, rice scented with saffron, flatbread brushed with ghee.

The food was beautiful. The kind of meal that should have grounded her.

Instead, every flavor arrived through a haze.

She tasted cardamom in the chai and thought of morning. She tasted smoke in the bread and thought of his clothes. Around her, the other guests spoke quietly, their conversations polite, their laughter soft. Elara answered when she was spoken to. She smiled. She performed normal well enough that no one would have known.

But inside, she was listening for what wasn't there.

After dinner, she carried a cup of tea back toward her tent and sat with her notebook open in her lap.

She wrote: I stayed where I was told to stay. That should feel like wisdom. Instead it feels like another kind of surrender.

She stared at the sentence. Then continued.

There are rules here I do not understand, but I can feel them pressing in from all sides. Arjun has not tried to keep me ignorant because I am a woman. He has tried to keep me from danger because he understands its shape. Because he belongs to it.

She crossed out nothing. Contradictions deserved to remain.

Her editor's message had arrived that afternoon, weak signal, barely legible: Hope India is spectacular. Need early selects if possible. Deadline still stands.

She had replied: India is extraordinary. I'll send selects soon.

Simple. Safe. True enough.

She put the phone away and did not think about New York.

Sleep came late and lightly.

When it did, she dreamed of a camel moving through darkness without a rider, without rope, without bells. It carried something hidden against its side, something she could feel but not see. Then it lowered itself into the sand and disappeared — shape, then shadow, then nothing.

She tried to call out.

No sound came.

Then Arjun's voice, from somewhere behind her: You cannot finish this story.

She turned.

He was gone.

She woke with her heart beating too fast. The tent was dark. The camp silent. She sat up, breathing slowly until the dream loosened its grip, then reached for the cup of water beside the bed.

She did not go outside.

Not even then.

Especially not then.

She was still telling herself that when she heard it.

Footsteps.

Not Ravi's careful shuffle. Not the camp staff's purposeful movement. These footsteps slowed at the edge of the carpeted path nearest her tent and then stopped.

Elara did not move.

The flap was closed. She could see nothing.

But she knew.

She didn't know how she knew. Perhaps it was the quality of the silence that followed — the particular stillness of someone standing still on purpose. Perhaps it was the way her body recognized it before her mind caught up.

She rose from the bed. Crossed the tent in three steps. Lifted the flap.

He was there.

Not close. Not approaching. Standing at the very edge where the lantern light gave out and the desert began, his back half-turned, his face angled toward the fair.

He was not looking at her.

And yet.

She stood in the opening of her tent and did not speak. He did not turn. The wind moved between them, warm and dry, carrying nothing.

A minute passed.

Maybe less.

Then Arjun turned his head — not fully, only enough — and for a moment she could see his profile against the darkness. Still. Composed. Carrying something she could not name.

Then he walked away.

Back into the fair. Back into whatever the night required of him.

Elara stood in the entrance of her tent until the darkness had taken him completely.

Then she stepped back inside.

She did not sleep again.

In the morning, she would not be certain it had happened.

But her body knew.

And her body did not forget.

CHAPTER TWENTY-TWO

When the Desert Answers

Elara waited until the camp went quiet.

That was her first mistake.

Her second was believing quiet meant no one would notice.

The night had settled heavily over the tent camp, pressing its darkness against the canvas walls, dimming the last of the lantern glow until the paths outside looked less red than black. Dinner had ended. Voices had drifted away. The clink of plates and cups had stopped. Even the distant fair seemed to have lowered itself into secrecy.

She sat on the edge of her bed fully dressed.

Waiting.

Listening.

Trying not to move.

The notebook lay open beside her, though she had not written a word in nearly an hour. The pen rested diagonally across the page, abandoned over a sentence she had started and could not finish.

If I go, I make it worse.

Below it, she had written nothing.

Because the sentence after that was the one she could not bring herself to put on paper.

If I don't go, I may never know what happened.

Ravi had told her Arjun was not hurt.

She believed him.

Mostly.

But mostly was not enough.

Not after the way Ravi's face had changed. Not after the older woman's warning. Not after the men who had watched her as if she had become a problem.

Some men are angry.

Because of many things.

You are one thing.

Elara closed the notebook.

Her hands were steady.

That surprised her.

Inside, she felt anything but steady.

She waited another minute. Then another. Outside, the wind moved lightly along the tent, brushing the canvas in soft, uneven strokes. Somewhere beyond camp, a camel gave a low, throaty call that lifted and fell into the dark.

She stood.

No camera this time.

That was the only compromise she made with herself.

No camera.

No notebook.

No evidence.

Only her body moving through the night.

She wrapped the dark cloth around her shoulders and lifted the tent flap.

The air outside was cool enough to raise goosebumps along her arms. The camp looked almost unreal beneath the low lanterns, too beautiful, too arranged, too temporary. Carpets stretched between the tents like ceremonial paths, their patterns softened by sand that had crept in during the day.

Elara stepped out barefoot first, then slipped into her sandals at the edge of the rug.

She paused.

Listened.

Nothing.

She moved.

Each step seemed louder than it should have. The faint brush of fabric. The soft press of leather against sand. Her own breathing.

She kept to the edge of the camp, where the lanterns thinned and the darkness gathered more completely. She knew the path now. That frightened her a little.

How quickly the forbidden becomes familiar.

She passed the last tent.

The carpet ended.

The sand began.

For a moment, she stopped at the boundary.

The fair lay ahead, mostly dark now, scattered with pockets of firelight and low lanterns that trembled in the wind. By day, it had been impossible to understand all at once. By night, it became something else entirely. Not smaller. Deeper.

The darkness did not hide the fair.

It revealed its other face.

Elara stepped forward.

The sand was cool beneath her sandals, loose and shifting. It pulled at each step, slowing her, making the body work harder than it expected. Dust rose faintly around her feet, less visible now, more felt than seen.

She stayed low in her movement, though she knew that was absurd. She was not trained for secrecy. She was not part of this world. Every step she took probably announced her.

Still, she moved.

The first section of the fair was quiet. Working camels rested in dark shapes, folded beneath themselves like strange monuments. A man slept near one of them, wrapped in cloth, his face turned away from the wind. A small fire burned low beside a cart, the embers pulsing red through ash.

She passed slowly.

A scent lingered in the night air.

Smoke.

Animal warmth.

Old rope.

Cooling spice from food fires now reduced to coals.

Then something sharper.

Fear, she thought.

But fear had no scent.

Or perhaps it did, and the desert had taught her to recognize it.

She moved farther.

The decorated section had changed most of all. During the day, it had been color, pride, spectacle. Now the fabrics were muted, their bright reds and oranges swallowed by night. The bells on the camels were silent. The animals stood or rested without ornament in the dark, their painted markings only faint patterns beneath the lantern glow.

Beyond that lay the place she had promised herself she would not go.

The quieter section.

She stopped before entering it.

Her body knew.

Every instinct in her body knew.

Do not go farther.

For once, the warning did not sound like fear.

It sounded like wisdom.

She almost turned back.

Then she heard a voice.

Low.

Angry.

Male.

Not close enough to understand, but close enough to recognize the tone.

She moved toward it.

The ground dipped slightly. She followed the slope of sand toward a cluster of low shapes at the edge of the section, where several camels stood near a darkened tent and a small fire shielded by stones.

There were men there.

Four, maybe five.

She saw their outlines first. Shoulders. Turbans. The movement of hands. One man stood apart from the others, facing them.

Arjun.

Her heart seemed to stop before it began pounding harder.

He stood still, but not relaxed. His body held tension in a way she had not seen before. His arms were at his sides. His head was slightly lowered as one of the older men spoke to him, the words quick and quiet and sharp.

The elder was there too.

The man in the pale turban.

He stood beside the fire, his face lit from below, the shadows carving deep lines into his cheeks.

Elara crouched instinctively behind the low edge of a cart.

The movement startled her as much as anything else.

She had never hidden from a story before.

Not like this.

The men continued speaking. She understood none of the words, but the meaning traveled clearly enough.

Accusation.

Warning.

Authority.

Arjun answered once, his voice lower than the others, steadier.

The elder interrupted him.

Another man stepped closer.

Elara's fingers curled around the rough wooden edge of the cart. Splinters pressed into her palm.

She could not hear everything. Only fragments of sound. A name she thought might be hers. A hard laugh from one of the younger men. Then Arjun's voice, sharper now.

The younger man moved toward him.

Elara's breath caught.

Arjun did not step back.

The man said something close to his face.

The elder lifted a hand.

The younger man stopped.

Barely.

The elder spoke again.

This time, slowly.

Arjun listened.

Then looked toward the camp.

Elara froze.

For one impossible second, she thought he saw her.

He couldn't.

The shadows were too deep. She was crouched low, hidden behind the cart, wrapped in dark cloth.

But his gaze held there.

Toward the exact place where she was.

Then his expression changed.

Not visibly to the others, perhaps.

But she saw it.

He knew.

A chill went through her.

The elder noticed the shift.

He turned.

Elara dropped lower, heart hammering now, the sand cold beneath one hand.

For several seconds, nothing happened.

Then footsteps.

Not toward her.

Away.

The voices shifted. The argument broke apart into smaller sounds. Men moving. Rope being handled. A camel groaning as it was pulled to its feet.

Elara dared to lift her head.

The group had begun to disperse.

Arjun was no longer among them.

Relief and panic struck at the same time.

Where had he gone?

A hand closed around her wrist.

She nearly cried out, but another hand covered her mouth before the sound escaped.

Arjun.

He crouched beside her, his face close, his eyes darker than the night around them.

Do not speak.

He did not say it.

He didn't have to.

His hand remained over her mouth only long enough for her to understand. Then he released her and pulled her behind the cart, deeper into shadow.

Her breath came too fast.

He leaned close, his voice barely air.

"What have you done?"

The anger in him was quiet.

That made it worse.

"I had to know," she whispered.

His eyes flashed.

"No."

The word was so low it barely sounded.

"You had to obey one thing. One thing."

She flinched.

Not because he was wrong.

Because he was right.

A rope dragged somewhere nearby. Men spoke in low bursts. A camel shifted, its feet pressing heavily into sand.

Arjun gripped her wrist again, not painfully, but firmly enough that she felt the force of his fear.

"Move when I move," he said.

She nodded.

He waited.

Listening.

The night seemed to stretch, every sound magnified.

Then he pulled her up.

They moved quickly, low and close, following the shadow of the cart until it ended near a stack of bundled cloth. Arjun paused there, then guided her behind a narrow line of tethered camels. The animals stood silent and enormous, their bodies warm even in the cool air, their scent surrounding her.

Dust.

Hide.

Breath.

She could feel one exhale near her shoulder, damp warmth brushing the night air.

Arjun moved like he belonged to darkness. He knew where to step, when to stop, when to pull her closer, when to hold still. Elara followed because she had no choice, and because for the first time since arriving, she understood fully that curiosity had limits.

They reached a deeper shadow beyond the last camel.

The camp lights were visible in the distance.

Too far.

A voice called out behind them.

Elara stopped breathing.

Arjun pulled her against him, pressing them both into the shadowed side of a low canvas shelter. His body shielded hers from view, one arm braced near her shoulder, his head turned slightly toward the sound.

She stood completely still.

The closeness was not romantic now.

It was survival.

And still, her body knew his.

That frightened her more than the men.

A lantern lifted in the distance.

Light moved across the sand.

Slowly.

Searching.

Arjun did not move.

Elara could hear his breathing, controlled and quiet. She tried to match it. Tried to become as still as he was.

The lantern light passed over the camels.

Over the cart.

Over the place where she had hidden moments before.

Then stopped.

A man said something.

Another answered.

A long pause followed.

Elara felt Arjun's hand close lightly around her shoulder.

Not comfort.

Instruction.

Stay.

The lantern shifted again.

Moved away.

The voices receded.

Only when the darkness settled fully did Arjun move.

He pulled back just enough to look at her.

His face was very close.

Anger, fear, and something more painful moved across his expression before he locked it away.

"You do not understand danger," he said.

His voice was barely a whisper.

She swallowed.

"I'm sorry."

The words were too small.

They both knew it.

He looked toward the camp.

"We go now."

This time, she obeyed without question.

They moved fast.

Not running.

Running would draw attention.

But quick enough that the distance to camp seemed both impossibly long and suddenly too short.

The sand dragged at her feet. Her lungs burned from holding fear too tightly. Every sound behind them felt like pursuit, though no one followed.

When they reached the edge of camp, Arjun did not stop.

He guided her past the first row of tents, past the dining canopy, past the low lanterns.

Only when they reached her tent did he release her wrist.

Elara turned to him, breathless.

The lantern outside her tent lit half his face, leaving the other half in shadow.

For the first time since she had met him, he looked shaken.

Not weak.

Never that.

But shaken.

And because of her.

"I'm sorry," she said again.

His jaw tightened.

"Do not say that if you do not understand what you almost did."

The words struck like a slap.

She deserved them.

"What did I almost do?"

His expression hardened.

"You almost made them decide you are not leaving soon enough."

A cold silence followed.

Elara felt the meaning unfold inside her slowly.

Not leaving soon enough.

Her throat went dry.

"They would hurt me?"

Arjun's eyes held hers.

"They would make sure you left."

The distinction was worse.

"And you?"

He looked away.

Only briefly.

But enough.

"They would make sure I remembered my place."

The words emptied the air from her lungs.

She stepped back, one hand finding the edge of the tent opening behind her.

"Because of me."

"Because I allowed you too close."

The answer hurt.

Because it carried responsibility in both directions.

"You didn't allow anything," she said, though her voice was weaker now. "I made my own choices."

"Yes," he said. "And I made mine."

The silence that followed was unbearable.

The camp around them slept, or pretended to. Somewhere a lantern flickered. The wind moved softly through the carpets, lifting the edges just enough to remind her that everything here was temporary.

Even safety.

Especially safety.

Arjun looked at her then, and the anger in his face gave way to something more devastating.

"You cannot come back from every line you cross," he said.

Elara felt tears sting unexpectedly behind her eyes.

Not from fear.

From the truth of it.

"I know."

"No," he said, softer now. "You are learning."

That broke something in her.

Because he was right.

She was still learning the same lesson in every country, every city, every version of desire.

You cannot fix this by going closer.

You cannot make wanting safe.

You cannot turn danger into love simply because it finally looks back.

"I thought if I saw enough, I would understand," she said.

Her voice shook this time.

"And now?"

She looked at him.

"Now I understand that seeing can be selfish."

His expression changed.

Barely.

But it changed.

He looked at her for a long moment.

Then stepped closer.

Not enough to touch.

Enough to make the air between them shift.

"You are not selfish," he said.

The words were quiet.

She almost laughed, but it came out as a breath.

"You don't know that."

"I know enough."

There it was again.

But tonight, it did not feel like arrogance.

It felt like mercy.

Elara looked down at his hand.

The same hand that had covered her mouth. Held her wrist. Pulled her through darkness. Shielded her against his own body.

She could still feel the imprint of it.

Not bruising.

Memory.

"I scared you," she said.

He did not answer.

That was answer enough.

She looked up.

"I did."

His eyes held hers.

"Yes."

The honesty moved through her more deeply than anger.

"I didn't think of that," she whispered.

"No."

"And you did."

"I think of many things you do not."

This time, the words did not irritate her.

They humbled her.

She nodded slowly.

"I won't go back there alone again."

"No," he said.

Not agreement.

Command.

She almost smiled through the tears she refused to let fall.

"No," she repeated. "I won't."

For a moment, the night softened around them.

Not safe.

Never safe.

But quieter.

Arjun lifted his hand.

Slowly.

For one suspended second, she thought he would touch her face.

She wanted him to.

She hated that she wanted him to.

His hand stopped before reaching her.

Then lowered.

Again, restraint.

Always restraint.

But now she understood the cost of it.

"Go inside," he said.

His voice was rougher than before.

She nodded.

Then hesitated.

"What happens to you now?"

He looked toward the dark beyond camp.

"Nothing tonight."

"And tomorrow?"

A pause.

"Tomorrow will ask its own price."

The words made her ache.

"Arjun."

He looked back at her.

She wanted to say too many things.

Stay.

Forgive me.

I'm afraid for you.

I'm afraid of myself.

Instead, she said, "Thank you."

Something in his face shifted.

Not enough to be called softness.

But enough for her to feel it.

Then he turned.

This time, she let him go.

She stepped inside the tent and lowered the flap behind her, but she did not move away from the entrance. She stood with her hand against the canvas, listening as his footsteps receded into the night.

Only when she could no longer hear them did she release the breath she had been holding.

The tent was the same as before.

The bed.

The table.

The notebook.

The camera she had left behind.

But she was not the same woman who had walked out.

She moved to the table and opened the notebook with trembling hands.

For a long time, she stared at the page.

Then she wrote:

Tonight the desert answered me.

She stopped.

Listened to the silence.

Then continued.

It said that not all truths are mine to enter. Not all doors are invitations. Not all danger becomes meaningful because I feel drawn to it.

Her hand paused.

Then one more line.

And not every man who saves you can be yours.

The words blurred slightly.

She closed the notebook before the tears could fall onto the page.

Outside, the desert returned to silence.

But now she knew better.

Silence did not mean nothing was happening.

It meant the desert had decided, for the moment, not to speak.

CHAPTER TWENTY-THREE

The Distance They Choose

The morning did not forgive her. Elara felt it the moment she stepped outside the tent. Not in any obvious way. The sky was still soft with early light. The camp moved with its usual quiet efficiency. Tea was carried on trays. Water was placed at tent doors. Voices remained low, respectful, measured. Everything appeared the same. But it wasn't. She could feel it in the air. A subtle shift. The way conversation paused half a second longer when she passed. The way eyes did not linger, but also did not ignore. The way space adjusted around her without acknowledging why. It was not hostility. It was awareness. And awareness here was more dangerous.

Elara walked slowly toward the dining canopy, her body more conscious of itself than it had been the day before. The cloth at her shoulders felt heavier. The camera against her chest felt louder, as if it carried weight beyond its size. She took tea. She sat. She ate. Normal. She forced herself into it. Because normal was the only protection she had left. Ravi approached halfway through her meal. He did not sit. That alone told her enough. "You should stay close to camp today," he said quietly. She didn't look up immediately. "I thought I already proved that I can't be trusted with that." Ravi's expression didn't change. "This is not punishment." "Then what is it?" "A chance." She looked at him then. "For what?" "For things to become smaller again." The words settled into her slowly. Smaller. As if what had happened could be reduced, folded back into something manageable, something forgettable. Elara shook her head slightly. "I don't think it works like that." "No," Ravi said. "It does not. But people pretend it does. That is how they continue." She held his gaze. "And Arjun?" Ravi hesitated. Only slightly. But she saw it. "He is working." "That's not new." "No." "Is he… all right?" Ravi's answer came carefully. "He is where he should be." That wasn't reassurance. That was positioning. Elara felt the distance immediately. Not physical. Deliberate. "Is he staying away from me?" she asked. Ravi didn't answer. He didn't need to.

Elara spent the morning in the open sections of the fair. She did exactly what she was supposed to do. She photographed the visible world. The safe world. The acceptable world. A line of camels decorated in color and bells, their handlers standing proudly beside them. A woman adjusting the scarf around her child's head, her fingers gentle, practiced. A trader laughing as he counted money into his palm. Everything was beautiful. Everything was true. And none of it was the whole story. She did not look toward the quiet edge. Not once. She did not search for him. Not openly. But absence has its own presence. By midday, she felt it like a pressure beneath her skin. Where are you? The question came without permission.

She ignored it. She kept working. She moved through the fair with discipline now, with control, with a kind of distance she had not carried before. And still, she knew. He was there. Somewhere beyond what she was allowed to see.

It was late afternoon when she saw him. Not where she expected. Not in the distance. Not hidden. Across the open fair. Surrounded by men. Not in confrontation. Not exactly. But not at ease. He stood among them, speaking in low tones, his posture contained, his movements precise. The men around him listened. One interrupted. Another spoke over him. The exchange remained controlled, but the energy around it felt tight. Elara stopped walking. Her body reacted before her mind did. That's because of you. The thought landed hard. She should look away. She didn't. Arjun turned. Their eyes met across the space. And everything stilled. Not the fair. Not the movement. Only them. For one suspended moment, the distance between them felt louder than anything else. He didn't step toward her. He didn't acknowledge her. Not outwardly. But she saw it. The recognition. And then he looked away. Deliberately. As if she were no one. As if she had never stood in the dark with him. As if he had never held her still while danger moved past them. As if none of it had happened. Elara felt it like impact. Not anger. Something sharper. Understanding. This is what distance looks like here. Not softness. Not space. Erasure. She forced herself to move. To turn. To walk. Every step away from him felt heavier than the night before. Because this time, he was choosing it.

Back at camp, she sat alone outside her tent. The sun had lowered enough to soften the heat, the air shifting into something almost gentle. Lanterns had not yet been lit. The world existed in that fragile space between day and night, where everything felt temporarily suspended. Elara held her notebook but did not open it. She didn't need to write this. She could feel it. He's protecting you. The realization came slowly. And himself. And everyone else. By pretending you are nothing. Her throat tightened. Of course. This was the only way. The only way to undo what had almost been seen. The only way to make the men forget. The only way to make her safe again. And still, it hurt. Because part of her had believed something different. Not consciously. But deeply. That what existed between them could hold itself somehow against the world around it. That it mattered enough to remain visible. That it might survive being seen. She let out a slow breath. No. This is the reality. And this is the cost.

The lanterns were being lit when she heard footsteps behind her. She didn't turn immediately. She already knew. "Miss Quinn." Ravi. She closed her eyes briefly before looking up. "Yes?" "He asked me to tell you something." Her chest tightened. "Of course he did." Ravi's expression softened just slightly. "He said you must stay in the light tonight." Elara let out a small, humorless breath. "That sounds like him." Ravi didn't smile. "He also said this will pass if you let it." The words landed. Heavy. Final. Let it pass. Let it become nothing. Let it disappear. Elara nodded slowly. "Thank you." Ravi lingered for a moment. Then, quietly, "He does not want you to be hurt." The statement was simple. But it held everything. Elara looked down at her hands. "I know."

That night, she stayed. Truly stayed. Inside the lines. Inside the light. Inside the version of the story she could survive. But something in her had shifted permanently. Because now she understood something she had never fully faced before. Distance is not always absence. Sometimes it is the most deliberate act of care. And the most painful.

CHAPTER TWENTY-FOUR

Stay in the Light

The message came after dinner.

Not written.

Not spoken directly.

Carried.

Like everything here that mattered.

Elara was standing near the edge of the dining canopy, holding a small cup of tea she had barely touched, watching the lanterns sway in the evening wind. Around her, the camp moved in its practiced rhythm. Plates were cleared. Guests drifted toward their tents. The scent of saffron rice and roasted vegetables still lingered in the air, softened now by smoke and cooling sand.

She had stayed in the light all day.

Just as he had asked.

Not because she wanted to obey him.

Because she understood now that obedience and wisdom sometimes wore the same face.

Ravi approached quietly.

She knew before he spoke that something had changed.

"Miss Quinn," he said.

Elara turned.

His expression was calm, but not easy.

"Yes?"

He glanced once toward the darker edge of camp, then back to her.

"He asks if you will walk."

Her heart shifted before she could stop it.

"Who?"

Ravi gave her a look.

She almost smiled.

Almost.

"Now?" she asked.

"Yes."

"Where?"

Ravi's answer came carefully.

"Not far."

Not far.

In this place, that meant very little.

Elara looked toward the fair. Most of it had dissolved into shadow, though scattered lanterns marked the paths like small, watchful fires.

"Is it safe?"

Ravi did not answer immediately.

Then he said, "Safer than before."

It was not reassuring.

But it was honest.

Elara set the untouched tea down on a nearby table.

"All right."

Ravi nodded once and stepped aside.

She followed him past the dining canopy, along the carpeted path, beyond the last row of glowing tents. The air cooled as they moved, carrying the dry mineral scent of sand and the faint smoke of distant fires. The noise of camp softened behind them.

At the boundary, Ravi stopped.

Arjun stood beyond the last lantern.

Not fully in darkness.

Not fully in light.

Of course.

He was turned slightly away, his profile cut against the dim gold behind him. His dark hair moved faintly in the breeze. He wore a pale shirt, sleeves rolled, the fabric marked with dust as if the desert had touched him before she could.

Ravi said nothing more.

He turned and left.

Elara remained where she was.

For a moment, neither she nor Arjun moved.

Then he looked at her.

"You came," he said.

"You asked."

A pause.

"Yes."

The simplicity of that settled between them.

She stepped forward, stopping just before the carpet ended.

He noticed.

His gaze dropped briefly to her feet, then returned to her face.

"You said to stay in the light," she said.

"I did."

"And now you're standing in the dark."

"Not far from it."

"That sounds like something you would say."

Something nearly softened in his expression.

Nearly.

Then he turned.

"Walk with me."

This time, she hesitated.

Only briefly.

Then stepped off the carpet and onto the sand.

They walked parallel to the camp, not toward the hidden section, not toward the fair's deeper darkness. The lanterns remained visible to their left, close enough to remind her of safety, distant enough to make her aware that they had left it.

Arjun kept his pace slow.

She knew he was doing it for her.

The sand shifted beneath her feet, cooler now, pulling gently at each step. Above them, the sky had opened fully. Stars appeared in staggering number, sharper here than they ever were in New York, scattered across the darkness like something spilled from a hand.

Elara looked up.

The sight stopped her.

Arjun stopped too.

For a moment, she forgot the fair. The men. The danger. The impossible weight of what had begun between them.

The sky was vast enough to make everything human seem briefly small.

"God," she whispered.

Arjun looked at the sky, then at her.

"You do not see stars where you live?"

"Not like this."

"No."

She continued looking upward.

"In New York, the sky is never really dark."

"Then how do you know when the day has ended?"

The question was so simple, and so strangely beautiful, that she looked at him.

"We don't," she said. "Maybe that's the problem."

He held her gaze for a moment.

Then looked away.

They began walking again.

The silence between them was different tonight. Not easy, exactly. But chosen. Neither of them tried to fill it too quickly.

Elara could hear the small sounds of their movement. Sand shifting. Fabric brushing. His breathing, steady and low beside her. Somewhere beyond them, a camel called once into the night, and the sound seemed to move through the dark rather than across it.

Finally, she said, "Why did you ask me to walk?"

He did not answer immediately.

"I needed to see you."

The words were quiet.

Direct.

They entered her before she could prepare for them.

She stopped walking.

Arjun took one more step, then stopped too.

He did not turn around at first.

When he did, his face was partially shadowed, but she could see enough.

Enough to know he wished he had not said it.

Enough to know he meant it.

"That's not something you should say," she said softly.

"I know."

"Then why did you?"

A pause.

"Because silence is not always safer."

The answer moved through her like heat.

She looked back toward the camp. The lanterns glowed steadily in the distance, small islands of safety against the dark.

"You ignored me today," she said.

"Yes."

"It hurt."

His eyes returned to hers.

"I know."

That answer cut more than denial would have.

"You knew?"

"Yes."

"And you did it anyway."

"Yes."

She stared at him.

Anger rose, but it was tangled with something worse. Understanding.

"You're very good at that," she said.

"At what?"

"Doing the thing that hurts because you think it's necessary."

He looked away.

For the first time, she saw that the words had landed.

"Yes," he said.

No defense.

No explanation.

Only truth.

The wind moved lightly between them, lifting the edge of her shawl. She held it down with one hand, suddenly aware of how exposed she felt even fully covered.

"I don't know how to do this," she said.

His gaze shifted back.

"Do what?"

"Stay away from something I want."

The words came out before she could stop them.

There they were.

Not dressed up as curiosity.

Not hidden behind the assignment.

Want.

Plain and dangerous.

Arjun's face changed.

Not much.

But enough.

He stepped closer, then stopped himself.

The restraint was visible now, and seeing it hurt more than if he had turned away.

"You think I do?" he asked.

The question was barely above a whisper.

Elara felt her breath catch.

The night seemed to hold completely still.

"No," she said.

A pause.

"I don't think you do."

They stood facing each other beneath the vast desert sky, the camp lights behind them, the fair shadows beyond them. Between the two worlds, exactly where neither of them should have been.

Arjun looked toward the lanterns.

"You leave soon."

She knew.

She hated hearing it.

"Yes."

"How soon?"

"Three days."

The words felt impossible.

Three days.

A measurement too small for something that had already changed her.

His jaw tightened.

He nodded once, as if he had expected it.

"And after?"

"Delhi. Then New York."

"Back to your life."

She almost laughed, but the sound stayed in her throat.

"I don't know what that means anymore."

He looked at her then.

"That is dangerous."

"What is?"

"When a visitor begins to believe she does not belong to the place she must return to."

The words hit too close.

Elara looked down at the sand.

"I didn't belong there before I came."

The admission surprised her.

Maybe because it was the closest she had come to saying the truth.

Arjun was silent.

So she continued.

"I had an apartment. Work. Friends. A life that looked like it should make sense. But I kept feeling like I was standing outside the window looking in."

She swallowed.

"And then I came here."

The rest did not need to be said.

He heard it anyway.

He always did.

"And now?" he asked.

She looked at him.

"Now I'm afraid I'll go back and nothing will fit."

For a moment, his expression softened in a way she had never seen so clearly.

Not pity.

Recognition.

"Some places do that," he said.

"They change you?"

"No."

His gaze held hers.

"They show you that you were already changing."

The words entered her slowly.

Settled.

Stayed.

Elara looked at him, truly looked, and felt the old instinct rise again. To believe that the man was the answer. To confuse the person with the awakening. To make him the doorway and the destination both.

But this time she saw it.

Saw herself reaching.

Saw the pattern forming before it became a cage.

She took one small step back.

Arjun noticed.

"What is it?"

She shook her head.

"I'm trying not to make you into something you're not."

His expression changed.

"And what am I?"

She looked at him for a long moment.

Dark hair. Shadowed eyes. Stillness. Danger. Tenderness held so tightly it almost looked like control.

"I don't know," she said. "That's the point."

A silence passed between them.

Then he nodded, slowly.

"That is wise."

She almost smiled.

"Don't sound so surprised."

This time, the faintest smile touched his mouth.

It was gone quickly, but she saw it.

And it undid her more than it should have.

They began walking again, slower now.

The camp remained beside them, close enough that they could be seen if someone looked carefully. Perhaps that was the point. This walk was not secret in the way last night had been secret. It was contained. Permitted, maybe. Or at least not hidden enough to be condemned.

That too felt like one of his compromises.

A narrow bridge between danger and need.

"Elara," he said after a while.

She looked at him.

"There is something I must tell you."

The tone of his voice shifted the night.

She felt it immediately.

"What?"

He walked a few steps farther before stopping.

She stopped too.

He looked toward the fair, where the darkness lay thicker.

"Tomorrow night, many of the camels will leave."

She waited.

He continued.

"Some for buyers. Some for villages. Some for places the fair does not name."

The words moved through her carefully.

"Drug routes."

He did not confirm with words.

He did not need to.

"And you?" she asked.

His silence answered first.

Then he said, "I go where I am expected."

The ground seemed to move beneath her.

"No."

The word came out instinctively.

Too quickly.

His gaze sharpened.

"You cannot say no to this."

"I just did."

"Elara."

"No. Don't say my name like that. Don't make it sound like I'm a child because I don't accept something terrible."

"This is not for you to accept."

The words struck hard.

She stepped back.

"Right."

His expression changed.

"That is not what I meant."

"Yes, it is."

"No."

"You keep reminding me I don't belong here, and then you ask me to walk with you, and then you tell me you're leaving tomorrow night for some dangerous route like I'm supposed to just nod because it isn't mine to understand."

His face tightened.

"It is not yours to stop."

"I know that."

"Do you?"

The question cut.

She opened her mouth, then closed it.

Because she didn't.

Not fully.

Some part of her still believed that wanting could intervene. That feeling something strongly enough could alter reality. That if she could make him see himself through her eyes, he might choose differently.

The old story.

The old mistake.

She looked away.

The stars above them remained impossibly bright.

"What happens if you don't go?" she asked.

His answer came quietly.

"Someone else pays."

She looked back at him.

The simplicity of it left no room for romance.

There was no noble escape. No dramatic refusal. No easy choice where love pulled him out of darkness and into light.

Only consequence.

Always consequence.

"Who?" she asked.

"My mother. My uncle. Men who work under me. People who trusted my father's name."

His father.

The inherited chain.

She felt the weight of it now.

"I didn't know," she said.

"No."

Not cruel.

Only true.

The anger left her as quickly as it had come.

In its place came something more painful.

Helplessness.

"I don't want you to go," she said.

This time the words were not impulsive.

They were quiet

Fully understood.

Arjun looked at her for a long moment.

"I know."

It hurt that he did.

It hurt that knowing changed nothing.

The wind moved through the space between them again, cooler now. Elara pulled the shawl closer around her shoulders.

"When?" she asked.

"After midnight."

"How long?"

"Two nights. Maybe three."

Three days until she left.

Two nights he might be gone.

The math was cruel.

"So I may not see you again."

He did not answer.

The silence opened beneath them.

She looked toward the camp, where the lanterns burned steadily, as if the world still believed in boundaries.

"This is why you asked me to walk."

"Yes."

"To tell me goodbye?"

His gaze held hers.

"To tell you the truth."

The difference mattered.

She hated that it mattered.

Elara felt something rise in her chest, something too large for the space inside her.

She wanted to be angry.

She wanted to plead.

She wanted to step into him and make the desert stop asking for things.

Instead, she stood still.

Maybe that was growth.

Maybe it was grief beginning early.

"What do you want from me?" she asked.

The question surprised him.

She could see it.

For once, he did not answer immediately.

The pause stretched long enough that she wondered if he would refuse the question entirely.

Then he said, "Nothing I should ask for."

Her breath caught.

"What does that mean?"

His face was very still.

"It means I wanted to see you before I left."

The words broke through her.

Softly.

Completely.

She looked at him.

The distance between them was small now. Not because either had moved closer, but because everything else had fallen away. The camp. The fair. The men who watched. The routes. The danger. The future.

For one suspended moment, there was only what they wanted and what they would not do with it.

Arjun reached for her then.

Slowly.

Not the way Luca had reached, with certainty that he would be received.

Arjun's hand lifted as if he understood the cost of every inch.

Elara did not move.

His fingers touched the edge of her shawl near her shoulder.

Not her skin.

Fabric.

Still, she felt it everywhere.

He adjusted the cloth gently where the wind had loosened it, drawing it more securely around her.

The gesture was intimate because it was not a claim.

Because it cared for the boundary instead of crossing it.

Elara's eyes stung.

He let his hand fall.

Neither spoke.

Then she stepped forward and closed the remaining space between them.

Not into his arms.

Not fully.

Just close enough that her forehead nearly touched his chest.

She stopped there, asking without words.

For a moment, he did nothing.

Then, slowly, he lowered his head until his brow rested lightly against hers.

No kiss.

No embrace.

Only that.

Breath shared in the narrow space between them.

The desert around them seemed to disappear and sharpen at once.

His skin was warm.

His breath steady, though she could feel the effort beneath it.

She closed her eyes.

This was worse than a kiss.

This required more restraint.

More feeling.

More truth.

“I will not ask you to stay,” he said.

His voice was so low she felt it more than heard it.

Her eyes remained closed.

“And I will not ask you not to go.”

A pause.

Then, softer, “Good.”

The word nearly broke her.

They remained like that for only a few seconds.

Or perhaps longer.

Time had stopped behaving properly.

Finally, Arjun stepped back.

The night returned.

The camp lights.

The sand.

The impossible line between them.

“You must go back now,” he said.

She nodded.

This time, she did not argue.

They walked in silence to the edge of the carpet.

When they reached it, Elara stopped.

He remained in the sand.

She remained on the edge of the light.

"Some distances are not meant to be crossed," she said quietly.

The words came without warning.

As if they had been waiting inside her.

Arjun looked at her.

For a moment, his face changed in a way she could not name.

Then he said, "But they are still felt."

She swallowed.

"Yes."

He held her gaze one last time.

Then turned toward the dark.

Elara watched him go.

This time, she did not call him back.

She did not ask him to stay.

She did not follow.

She stood in the light and let him walk toward the darkness that had claimed him long before she arrived.

Only when he was gone did she step back into camp.

In her tent, she opened her notebook with hands that did not tremble this time.

She wrote only one line.

The desert does not give you what you want. It shows you what wanting costs.

Then she closed the notebook.

Outside, the lanterns burned until the wind began to dim them one by one.

And somewhere beyond the last safe light, Arjun Rathore prepared to leave.

CHAPTER TWENTY-FIVE

The Leaving

She did not see him leave.

That was the first thing the morning gave her.

Not light.

Not sound.

Absence.

Elara woke before dawn with the sense that something had already happened. The tent was dim, the canvas walls holding the last of the night in soft gray folds. For a moment, she lay completely still, listening for anything that might prove otherwise.

Footsteps.

Voices.

A camel groaning in the dark.

His name carried by someone outside.

Nothing came.

Only the faint brush of wind against canvas and the distant, low stirring of a fair beginning another day without asking permission from anyone's heart.

She sat up slowly.

The air inside the tent was cool, touched by the dry mineral scent of sand. Her notebook lay closed on the table where she had left it. The camera beside it. The shawl folded over the chair, still carrying the faint shape of where he had adjusted it against her shoulder.

Elara looked at it for too long.

Then she stood.

Outside, the camp had not yet fully woken. The lanterns along the red carpets had burned low, their flames small and tired inside glass. The sky above the desert was beginning to pale, not blue yet, not gold, only a quiet thinning of darkness.

The world felt suspended.

She stepped out barefoot and stood on the carpet, letting the cold woven threads press into her skin.

Beyond the camp, the fair was shadow and shape.

Somewhere out there, after midnight, Arjun had left.

No farewell.

No last look.

No dramatic turning back beneath the stars.

Only departure.

The way men like him survived.

The way men like him kept others safe.

The way men like him broke your heart without ever promising not to.

Elara wrapped her arms around herself and looked toward the dark edge of the desert.

She did not cry.

Not then.

The feeling inside her was too quiet for tears.

Too vast.

She had thought absence would arrive like pain.

Sharp.

Immediate.

Instead, it arrived like weather.

Everywhere at once.

By the time hot water was placed at her tent door, the sun had begun to rise.

The man who brought it nodded, as always, and disappeared along the carpeted path. Elara thanked him too late, her voice barely carrying. She stood for a moment looking at the brass vessel, steam lifting faintly from its mouth into the cool morning air.

The ritual that had once charmed her now felt almost unbearably tender.

Hot water brought to the door.

Tea carried by hand.

Food prepared before the day grew harsh.

Care offered quietly, without spectacle.

This place had been full of such details from the beginning. She had noticed them, photographed some, written others down. But now they seemed to gather meaning differently.

Because she understood that care here was not always soft.

Sometimes care was a warning.

Sometimes care was silence.

Sometimes care was a man walking into darkness without letting you follow.

She bathed slowly, as if the day required preparation. The water cooled as she used it, slipping over her arms, her shoulders, her neck. Dust lifted from her skin, clouding the basin in pale swirls.

But not everything washed away.

Not the memory of his hand at her wrist.

Not the warmth of his brow resting against hers.

Not the words spoken at the edge of the light.

Some distances are not meant to be crossed.

But they are still felt.

She closed her eyes.

There it was.

The title of the ache.

The thing she would carry, whether she wanted to or not.

Breakfast was quieter than usual.

Or perhaps she heard it differently.

Guests moved through the dining canopy with the sleep-thick politeness of travelers. Cups were filled. Plates set down. Someone discussed a sunrise camel ride. Someone else asked whether the fair would be as busy today as it had been yesterday.

Elara sat alone with chai and flatbread, the food fragrant and warm before her.

She tore off a piece of bread and dipped it into spiced potatoes bright with turmeric and cumin. The flavor was beautiful. Earthy, sharp, comforting.

She chewed slowly.

Swallowed with effort.

Across the canopy, Ravi stood speaking to one of the camp staff. He glanced toward her once. Only once.

Then looked away.

That told her enough.

He knew Arjun was gone.

He knew she knew.

He also knew better than to say it before she asked.

When he finally approached, she was stirring her chai though there was nothing left to stir.

"Miss Quinn," he said.

She looked up.

"Good morning, Ravi."

"Good morning."

He stood for a moment, hands loosely clasped in front of him.

The silence between them was careful.

She decided to break it.

"He left."

Ravi's face remained composed.

"Yes."

The word landed softly.

Still, it landed.

"When?"

"Late."

"After midnight?"

"Yes."

She looked down at the cup.

"Did he go safely?"

Ravi hesitated.

Not long.

Long enough.

"He left as expected."

That was not the same thing.

Elara let out a slow breath.

"And that is the best answer you can give me?"

"For now."

She nodded.

The restraint required not to ask more felt physical.

"Will he come back before I leave?"

Ravi did not answer.

This time, the pause stretched.

Elara looked up.

"Ravi."

"I do not know."

The truth entered her quietly.

She had known it already.

Still, hearing it made the world tilt.

She looked toward the edge of the canopy, where the morning light had begun to warm the sand beyond camp.

"All right," she said.

Ravi's expression softened.

"I am sorry."

The words surprised her.

Not because they were unkind.

Because they were.

Sorry.

Plainly.

Humanly.

Elara's throat tightened.

"For what?"

"For what this place gives and takes."

She tried to smile, but failed.

"That sounds like something he would say."

Ravi almost smiled.

"He has learned from the desert."

"And you?"

Ravi looked toward the fair.

"I have learned from watching people misunderstand it."

The words were gentle.

They still cut.

Elara nodded.

"I suppose I've given you a lot to watch."

"Yes," he said.

There was no cruelty in it.

Only honesty.

Then he added, "But you are watching yourself now. That is different."

She looked at him.

The words struck deeper than she expected.

Before she could respond, Ravi stepped back.

"You should go today," he said.

"To the fair?"

"Yes. But stay where there is light."

She almost laughed.

The phrase had become part of her now.

Stay in the light.

"I will."

This time, she meant it.

The fair had begun to empty.

Not dramatically.

Not enough for someone arriving fresh to notice.

But Elara saw it.

Spaces had opened where there had been none the day before. Clusters of camels had thinned. Some of the decorated animals were gone, leaving flattened patches in the sand where they had knelt, their absence marked by rope impressions, trampled earth, and scattered bits of colored thread.

Carts moved slowly away from the center of the fair, loaded with rolled blankets, brass pots, bundles of fabric, children half asleep atop sacks of grain. Men who had shouted prices days earlier now spoke in quieter tones, the urgency of buying replaced by the fatigue of leaving.

The fair was not ending all at once.

It was loosening.

Unmaking itself.

Elara moved through it with her camera, but slowly.

Today, every photograph felt like a farewell.

Click.

A man folding a bright cloth that had decorated a camel's back.

Click.

A child sleeping in a cart beside a bundle of rope.

Click.

A line of camels walking west, their silhouettes dissolving into dust.

The air tasted different too.

Less crowded with food and movement.

More sand.

More distance.

Wind lifted fine grains into the morning light, and they shimmered briefly before settling on everything. Her camera. Her sleeves. Her lips.

She did not wipe them away.

Let the desert leave proof, she thought.

She did not know where the thought came from.

Perhaps from him.

Perhaps from herself.

Perhaps there was no longer a clean difference.

She stayed in the open sections.

Working camels.

Families.

Traders.

Visible departures.

And yet the hidden world remained present because of what it had taken from the frame.

There were places she did not look.

Places she would not photograph.

Men she would not follow.

That too had become part of her work.

The restraint.

The empty space.

The story not taken.

At midday, she sat beneath a patch of shade near a food stall and reviewed a few images. Her editor would love them. The fair looked ancient and alive, intimate and sweeping. Human and vast.

A publishable truth.

Not the whole truth.

But perhaps no photograph ever was.

She paused on one image.

A camel's face in close frame, lashes dark, eye calm and reflective. In the reflection, almost too small to see, was a distorted shape of the fair. Light. Sand. A woman holding a camera.

Her.

She stared at it for a long time.

For once, she was inside the image and outside it.

Observer and observed.

The woman who took.

The woman who had learned not to.

She turned the camera off.

In the afternoon, the older woman found her again.

Elara was standing near a row of camels being prepared for departure when she felt someone beside her. She turned and saw the woman in the blue sari, the same faded gold border catching the light.

For a moment, they said nothing.

Then the woman looked toward the camels.

"Many go today."

Elara nodded.

"Yes."

The woman's gaze remained forward.

"Men go also."

Elara's breath caught.

She said nothing.

The woman looked at her then, direct as ever.

"You did not go after him."

It was not a question.

Elara swallowed.

"No."

"Good."

The single word landed with unexpected weight.

Not approval, exactly.

Acknowledgment.

Elara looked down at her hands.

"I wanted to."

"Yes."

No surprise.

No judgment.

Only recognition.

The woman adjusted the edge of her sari over her shoulder.

"When heart is hungry, it thinks every fire is food."

Elara looked at her.

The words moved through her slowly, finding places she had not known were open.

The woman continued.

"Some fire cooks. Some fire burns house."

Elara almost smiled through the ache in her chest.

"That seems like something I should have learned a long time ago."

The woman's expression did not change.

"Learning comes when it comes."

Then she reached out and touched the edge of Elara's shawl, adjusting it slightly at her shoulder the way she had once covered her legs.

The gesture undid her.

Not because it was dramatic.

Because it was not.

It was care without demand.

Correction without humiliation.

A blessing without being named.

"Go home with eyes open," the woman said.

Elara's throat tightened.

"I'm trying."

The woman nodded.

Then, as before, she left without ceremony, disappearing into the movement of the fair.

Elara stood there a long time after.

When heart is hungry, it thinks every fire is food.

She repeated it silently, letting the words settle into memory.

Luca had been fire.

Arjun was fire too.

Different flame.

Different heat.

But fire nonetheless.

And she was finally old enough, or wounded enough, or awake enough to stop pretending that being drawn to warmth meant she was meant to step into it.

Near sunset, she returned to camp.

The day had left her covered in dust. It clung to the hem of her skirt and gathered in the fine lines of her hands. Her hair felt dry and wind-tangled. Her lips tasted of salt and sand.

She was tired in a way sleep would not repair.

At the entrance to her tent, she found something waiting.

A folded piece of cloth.

Deep red.

Threaded with gold.

For a moment, she did not move.

The world narrowed to that square of color resting on the low wooden stool beside her tent door.

Red and gold.

The fabric caught the last light of day and held it.

Her heart began to pound.

She looked around.

No one stood nearby.

No note.

No explanation.

Only the sari.

Elara stepped closer slowly, as if the cloth might vanish if she moved too quickly.

She touched it with two fingers.

Soft.

Heavier than expected.

The gold thread was raised slightly, textured beneath her fingertips, intricate and beautiful in a way that made her chest hurt. She lifted it carefully, unfolding just enough to see the pattern. Flowers, vines, small mirrored accents stitched into the border, catching light like tiny fragments of sun.

She knew.

She did not know how she knew.

But she did.

This was from him.

Not a promise.

Not a claim.

A recognition.

A farewell, perhaps.

Or worse.

Something without a name.

She pressed the cloth lightly against her chest before she could stop herself.

Then lowered it quickly, as if embarrassed before witnesses who were not there.

Inside the tent, she laid it across the bed.

The red seemed impossibly vivid against the pale bedding.

Too alive.

Too intimate.

Too much.

She sat beside it.

For a long time, she did not touch it again.

Then she did.

Her fingers traced the gold border slowly.

She thought of the woman's words.

Some fire cooks. Some fire burns house.

She thought of Arjun adjusting her shawl.

Of his brow against hers.

Of his voice in the dark.

I wanted to see you before I left.

The ache came then.

Not sharp.

Deep.

She bent forward, one hand covering her mouth.

This time, she cried.

Quietly.

Not for long.

But fully.

For the man who had gone.

For the woman she had been.

For the girl in New York who had thought being chosen by danger meant she had won something.

For the truth that love, or whatever this was, did not always arrive to be lived.

Sometimes it arrived to reveal.

When the tears passed, she sat very still.

Outside, the camp moved toward evening. Lanterns were lit. Voices softened. Somewhere, dinner was being prepared, and the air filled again with cumin, ginger, coriander, and smoke.

Life continued with almost unbearable tenderness.

Elara opened her notebook.

She did not write about the sari.

Not directly.

Instead, she wrote:

He left me something beautiful that I cannot wear.

She stared at the sentence.

Then added:

Maybe that is the lesson.

Her hand hovered.

Then one more line:

Not everything given in love is meant to become a life.

She closed the notebook.

The sari remained beside her, red and gold in the dimming light.

A piece of a world that was not hers.

A gift she should perhaps refuse.

A gift she knew she would keep.

That night, she did not go to the dining canopy.

Food was brought to her tent. A simple tray. Lentils, rice, bread, tea. She ate sitting beside the sari, tearing pieces of bread slowly, tasting very little.

Afterward, she stepped outside.

The desert was dark now.

The fair quieter than it had been since her arrival. More spaces empty. More fires extinguished. The night felt larger because there was less human noise to hold it back.

Elara stood at the edge of the carpet with the shawl wrapped around her shoulders.

She did not look for him.

For the first time, not looking was not discipline.

It was acceptance.

He was gone.

The desert had taken him into the part of itself she could not follow.

She looked up.

The stars were fierce and endless.

In New York, the sky never truly darkened.

Here, darkness was not absence.

It was depth.

She stood there until the cool air settled through her clothing and into her skin.

Then she whispered, though no one was there to hear it.

"Come back safely."

The words disappeared into the desert.

No answer came.

But she had not expected one.

Behind her, inside the tent, the red and gold sari lay across the bed like an ember that would not go out.

Elara turned back toward it.

Tomorrow, she would begin deciding what to take home.

And what to leave unnamed in the sand.

CHAPTER TWENTY-SIX

What You Keep, What You Leave

The desert was quieter the next day. Not silent. Never silent. But altered. Elara felt it as soon as she stepped outside her tent. The fair had begun its slow unraveling. Where there had once been tight clusters of camels, there were now open pockets of sand. Where men had argued over prices, there were now conversations about departure. The energy had shifted from arrival to leaving, from anticipation to completion, from wanting to carrying. She stood for a moment at the edge of the red carpet, the morning light soft against her face, and let herself feel it fully. The difference. The absence. The weight of what remained.

Inside her tent, the sari waited. Red. Gold. Unavoidable. She had not folded it. Not yet. It lay exactly where she had left it the night before, stretched across the bed like something still alive. She did not touch it.

Instead, she reached for her camera. Today was not about the fair. Not entirely. Today was about what she had taken and what she would do with it. She sat at the small table, the camera in her hands, and turned it on. The screen lit up. Her work. Days of it. Color. Movement. Faces. Animals. Light. Dust suspended in air like something sacred. She began to scroll.

A wide shot of the fair at sunrise. Endless camels, long shadows stretching across pale sand. Beautiful. Publishable. Safe. A close portrait of a woman laughing, her teeth bright against sun-darkened skin, her scarf pulled loosely around her head. Human. Warm. True. A child asleep in a cart, his hand curled around a piece of rope as if it were something precious. Tender. Intimate. Perfect. She continued. The working camels. The decorated camels. The traders. The food stalls. Everything her editor had asked for. Everything that would make the story land. Then she stopped.

A different set of images appeared. Not many. But enough. She hadn't meant to take them. Or perhaps she had. The edge of the fair. The quiet section. The men who did not perform for the camera. The camels without ornament. And one image—the one she had not deleted. A shape in shadow. A man partially turned away. Not fully visible. Not identifiable to anyone who did not already know. But she knew. Arjun.

Elara's breath slowed. She stared at the image. Not because it was beautiful. Because it was dangerous. This is the truth. The thought rose immediately. And then—Is it yours? She leaned back in the chair. The camera rested in her lap. The question sat heavier than any she had asked herself before. She had always believed in truth, in showing what was real, in capturing the moments others overlooked. That was her work. Her purpose. Her identity. But this—this was different. Because this truth did not belong to a system, or a place, or an idea. It belonged to people. People who could not leave it behind. People who lived inside it. People who would pay for it if she chose to expose it.

Elara closed her eyes. Luca would have published it. The thought came uninvited. He would have loved the danger, the edge, the idea of being part of something illicit and hidden. He would have called it power. He would have called her fearless. He would have kissed her and told her she was brilliant for getting close enough to see it. And then he would have walked away untouched by whatever consequences followed. She opened her eyes. That is not who you are anymore. The realization didn't come as a declaration. It came as a quiet correction.

Elara lifted the camera again. Her thumb hovered over the image. Delete. Her heart beat harder. This is the story. No. This is a story. Not the story. She pressed the button. The image disappeared. She exhaled slowly. Not everything you can take belongs to you. His words. Her choice.

She continued. More images. More decisions. She removed anything that suggested more than it showed, anything that could lead someone closer to the places she had been told not to enter, anything that felt like theft instead of witnessing. It took time. More than she expected. Because each deletion felt like a negotiation between who she had been and who she was becoming. When she finished, the camera held a different story. Still beautiful. Still real. Still worthy. But contained. Respectful. Incomplete. And somehow more honest.

She set the camera down. Her hands were steady. Her chest felt lighter. Not empty. Clear. For the first time since arriving, she understood something she had never fully grasped before. Truth is not only what you reveal. It is what you choose to protect.

The sari waited. She turned toward it slowly. This time, she did not hesitate. She stood and crossed the small space of the tent, sitting beside it on the bed. Her fingers moved across the fabric, tracing the gold thread, feeling the slight raised texture of the embroidery beneath her skin. It was beautiful. Undeniably. Unquestionably. She lifted it. The weight surprised her again. Not heavy. But present. Like something meant to be worn with awareness. Elara held it in her lap. This is not yours. The thought came gently. And yet it had been given to her. Not as a promise. Not as a claim. As a moment. As a recognition of something that had existed, however briefly, between two people who would never build a life from it.

She folded it carefully. Not quickly. Not carelessly. Each movement deliberate. Respectful. When she finished, she placed it in her bag. Not hidden. Not displayed. Carried.

That afternoon, she returned to the fair one last time. Not to search. Not to hope. To see. The space where the hidden section had been felt emptier now. Not gone. Never gone. But less visible. Less accessible. As if the desert had closed something behind her. Good. She did not belong there. She understood that now. Not as rejection. As truth.

She walked through the open areas slowly, taking a few final photographs. Not many. She did not need them. What she needed, she already carried. The lesson. The pattern. The shift. As the sun lowered, she stood at the edge of the fair and looked out across the desert. The wind moved steadily now, lifting fine dust into the air, softening edges, blurring distance. Camels moved in long lines toward the horizon. Men walked beside them. Figures becoming shapes. Shapes becoming memory.

Elara felt it then. The difference between wanting and belonging. She had wanted him. Deeply. But she did not belong in his world. And he did not belong in hers. That did not make what existed between them less real. It made it complete. In a way that did not require continuation.

Back at camp, she packed slowly. Not everything. Just enough to begin. Tomorrow, she would leave. Delhi. Then New York. The life she had once questioned. The life she would now return to with different eyes. She paused at the edge of the tent and looked out one last time. The lanterns had been lit again. The same soft glow. The same quiet rhythm. But she was not the same woman standing in it.

She understood now: Not every fire is meant to be fed. Not every story is meant to be told. Not every love is meant to be lived. And that did not make them less important. It made them sacred.

CHAPTER TWENTY-SEVEN

The Story She Tells

Elara wrote the story the next morning. Not all at once. Not in a rush.

She began slowly, sitting at the small table inside her tent while the early light moved gently through the canvas walls, turning everything a soft, diffused gold. The camp was quieter now. Half the tents had already been taken down. The red carpets no longer stretched as far. Spaces had opened where there had once been symmetry, revealing the sand beneath in uneven patches. Even here, departure had begun. She opened her laptop. The screen felt almost foreign after days of working only through the lens of her camera and the pages of her notebook. A blinking cursor waited. Impatient. Expectant. Familiar. She stared at it for a long moment. Then she began.

Pushkar arrives slowly, not as a single place but as a gathering of movement across the desert. She paused. Read it again. Left it. She wrote about the camels. About the journey. About the men who traveled across miles of sand with animals that carried not just labor, but livelihood. She wrote about the colors. The rituals. The temporary city that rose and fell each year like something both ancient and fleeting. She wrote the truth. But not all of it. She described the sections of the fair without naming the invisible boundaries. She captured the difference between working animals and decorated ones, between spectacle and survival. She wrote about the way the desert shaped behavior. How silence carried meaning. How presence was negotiated through respect rather than force. Her words were precise. Measured. Clear. And still she felt the edges of what she was not writing.

The hidden section. The men in the shadows. The camels that moved at night. Him. Her fingers hovered above the keyboard. The cursor blinked. This is where you decide. She closed her eyes briefly. Then continued. There are parts of the fair that are not meant for visitors. Not because they are hidden, but because they belong to those who live within them. She stopped. Read it again. That was the closest she would come. Not a lie. Not an exposure. A boundary. She continued writing. She wrote about the people. The women who moved with quiet authority. The children who understood the rhythms of the desert before they could speak them. The men whose lives were shaped by inheritance, expectation, and survival. She did not romanticize them. She did not judge them. She let them exist.

When she finished the first draft, the sun had climbed high enough to warm the tent fully. The air inside had grown thick, holding both heat and the faint scent of dust carried in from outside. Elara leaned back in the chair. Read the story from the beginning. Then again. It was good. It would be well received. Her editor would call it evocative. Thoughtful. Immersive. And safe. The word settled into her. Safe. Not as an insult. As a choice. She saved the document. Attached the images she had selected. The ones she had chosen to keep. The ones she had chosen not to delete. The ones that told a story that was true without exposing what did not belong to her.

She hovered over the send button. Once she sent it, the story would no longer belong to her. It would move outward. Be read. Interpreted. Consumed. She thought of the hidden images she had deleted. The ones no one would ever see. The ones that would remain only in her memory. She thought of him. Not as a subject. Not as a story. As a person who would continue his life untouched by what she chose to publish. Her finger moved. She pressed send. The email disappeared. Just like that. The story she told the world was complete.

She sat in silence after. Not immediately relieved. Not immediately certain. Just still. Then she reached for her notebook. Opened it. Turned to a blank page. This time, what she wrote was not for anyone else. I told the truth. She paused. Then added: Just not all of it. She stared at the words. Let them settle. Then continued. There is a version of me that would have told everything, that would have chased the edge, captured the danger, and called it bravery. Her hand slowed. That version of me believed that getting close to something dangerous made it hers. She stopped. Looked at the page. Then, carefully, this version of me understands that not everything I am drawn to is mine to hold. Her chest tightened. Not with regret. With recognition.

She thought of Luca. The way she had mistaken intensity for depth. The way she had believed that if she stayed long enough, loved hard enough, proved herself worthy enough, something unstable would become stable. She thought of Arjun. The way he had never promised her anything. The way he had drawn lines instead of erasing them. The way he had stepped back when stepping forward would have been easier. She closed her eyes. You chose differently. The realization did not feel triumphant. It felt quiet. Earned. She wrote one more line. I did not follow him. She sat back. The words looked simple on the page. They were not.

Outside, the camp had begun to dismantle itself further. More tents were gone. The carpets rolled. The space widening. Returning to desert. Elara stepped outside. The light hit her fully now, the sun higher, sharper, less forgiving. The air had warmed enough that the scent of sand rose more strongly, dry and almost metallic beneath the faint traces of food and smoke. She walked slowly through what remained of the camp. Men worked efficiently, folding canvas, stacking supplies, preparing to leave no trace that they had ever been there. Temporary. All of it.

She stopped at the place where her tent had stood the day before. It looked smaller now. Less significant. That felt right. Ravi approached from the far side of the camp. She saw him before he reached her. He carried himself the same way as always—calm, observant, steady. “You are leaving tomorrow,” he said when he reached her. “Yes.” “And your work?” “It’s done.” He studied her face. “And you?” The question surprised her. She thought about it. Really thought. Then said, “I think I am too.” Ravi nodded slowly. “That is good.” A pause. Then, “Many people leave places without finishing what they came to understand.” She almost smiled. “I didn’t understand everything.” “No,” he said. “But you understood enough.” The words settled into her. Not praise. Not dismissal. Truth.

She hesitated. Then asked, “Have you heard from him?” Ravi’s expression did not change. “No.” The answer was simple. Expected. Still, something inside her tightened. She nodded. “Of course.” Ravi looked toward the desert. “He will return.” Not reassurance. Not a promise. Just a statement. Elara followed his gaze. The horizon stretched endlessly, the line between earth and sky blurred by distance and heat. "Yes," she said softly. "But not for me." Ravi did not answer. He didn't need to.

They stood there for a moment longer. Then he inclined his head slightly. "I wish you a safe journey." "Thank you." He turned and walked away. Elara remained, looking out at the desert. The same desert that had brought her here, that had shown her something she had not been ready to see, that had taken something from her and given something else in return. She did not feel empty. She did not feel full. She felt clear.

Behind her, the last of the camp shifted, preparing to disappear. Ahead of her, the desert waited, unchanged by her presence, unmoved by her departure. She turned back toward what remained of her things. Tomorrow, she would leave. Delhi. Then New York. The life she had questioned. The life she would now re-enter with a different understanding. She paused at the entrance to her tent. Then stepped inside. The bag was packed. The sari folded carefully within it. Her camera ready. Her notebook closed. Everything she would carry was chosen now. Not taken. Chosen.

She sat on the edge of the bed one last time. Looked around. Then whispered, though no one was there to hear it, "I'm ready." And for the first time since she arrived, she meant it.

CHAPTER TWENTY-EIGHT

The Road Back

The camp was almost gone by morning.

Elara stood outside her tent with her bag at her feet, watching men fold canvas that had once held whole rooms of light and shadow. The bed was gone. The small table was gone. The basin, the brass vessel, the lantern that had burned outside her entrance each night.

All of it had been lifted, carried, rolled, stacked.

The red carpets were disappearing too.

One by one, they were pulled from the sand, beaten lightly, then rolled into tight cylinders and carried away on narrow shoulders. Beneath them, the desert reappeared, marked only faintly by where they had been.

Temporary.

That was the final truth of the place.

The camp had never belonged to the desert.

It had only borrowed space from it.

And now the desert was taking it back.

Ravi stood beside the car, speaking with another man in low tones. When he saw her watching, he stepped forward.

"Are you ready, Miss Quinn?"

Elara looked once more toward the emptying fair.

There were still camels in the distance, but fewer now. The great gathering that had felt endless when she arrived had thinned into movement, departure, and dust. Lines of animals crossed the horizon in slow procession, each one led by men returning to villages, fields, markets, routes, lives.

Some would go where she could imagine.

Some would go where she could not.

She looked for him.

Not with her eyes.

With the part of her that had known when he was near before she saw him.

Nothing answered.

She nodded.

"Yes," she said. "I'm ready."

Ravi took her bag and placed it carefully in the car.

Before she stepped in, Elara turned back toward the camp one last time.

The place where her tent had stood was nearly bare now.

Only a square of slightly flattened sand remained.

She wanted to feel something dramatic.

A breaking.

A finality.

Instead, she felt quiet.

Not healed.

Not untouched.

Quiet.

As if something inside her had been rearranged while she was not looking, and now she had to learn the shape of herself again.

She climbed into the car.

Ravi closed the door.

A moment later, the engine started.

The camp receded slowly at first, then more quickly, the last canvas peaks shrinking behind them until they became pale shapes against the desert.

Then nothing.

Only sand.

Only light.

Only the road.

Elara did not look back again.

That surprised her.

More than leaving did.

The road out of Pushkar felt different from the road in.

When she had arrived, everything ahead had been unknown. The fair. The camp. The story. The man.

Now the same desert unfolded around her, but it carried memory in every direction.

A turn in the road where she had first seen a line of camels in the distance.

A roadside stall where she had tasted chai and felt the first warmth of cardamom on her tongue.

A stretch of open land where the horizon had seemed to pull her forward.

It was strange how quickly a place could become marked.

Not by years.

By feeling.

Elara sat in the back seat with her camera bag beside her and the red and gold sari folded carefully inside her luggage. She had placed it between layers of clothing, not hidden exactly, but protected.

The car windows were open just enough to let the air move through.

Dust entered with it.

Fine and pale.

It settled along the edge of the seat, on her wrist, in the creases of her fingers.

She let it.

Ravi drove in silence for the first hour.

She was grateful for that.

There were some departures that could not survive conversation too soon.

Outside, the desert shifted gradually from fairground to open road. Camels appeared occasionally, but now they were solitary or in small groups, no longer part of the vast spectacle that had overwhelmed her days before.

A man walked beside one, one hand resting lightly on the rope, his turban bright against the muted earth.

A woman stood near a well, lifting water with slow, practiced effort.

Children ran along the edge of the road, waving at the passing car.

Elara lifted her hand in return.

She did not lift her camera.

Not yet.

Some moments, she had learned, were meant only to pass through you.

After a while, Ravi spoke.

"You are very quiet today."

Elara looked toward the front seat.

"I think I'm tired."

"Yes," he said. "But not only tired."

She smiled faintly.

"You notice too much."

"I am a driver. That is my work."

"To notice?"

"To see who is in the car."

She let that settle.

Outside, the road stretched ahead, pale and shimmering beneath the morning sun.

"Did you know?" she asked.

Ravi glanced at her through the mirror.

"Know what?"

"That this trip would become something else."

His eyes returned to the road.

"No."

A pause.

"Maybe I knew it could."

"Why?"

"Because you looked like someone who was running from one life and not yet ready for another."

The words entered gently.

She looked out the window.

"Was I that obvious?"

"To some people."

"And to him?"

Ravi did not answer immediately.

Then he said, "Especially to him."

Elara closed her eyes for a moment.

Of course.

Arjun had seen that first.

Not because he loved her.

Not because he wanted her.

Because he understood what it meant to live between worlds.

"You think he'll be all right?" she asked.

Ravi kept his eyes on the road.

"He knows how to return."

"That isn't the same thing."

"No."

The honesty hurt less than false comfort would have.

She nodded.

The silence returned.

This time, it felt companionable.

They stopped near midday at a roadside place that appeared almost out of nowhere.

A few low tables beneath a patched awning. A man standing over a hot surface, pressing dough into flat rounds with practiced hands. A kettle steaming nearby. The smell reached Elara before she stepped out of the car.

Tea.

Ginger.

Toasted flour.

Oil.

Smoke.

The world had narrowed to travel and hunger.

Ravi ordered for them. Elara did not ask what it was. She trusted him now in the small ways that matter on a long road.

They sat at a metal table in the shade. The surface was warm beneath her palms. Dust had gathered at the edges, and someone had wiped the center clean with a damp cloth, leaving faint streaks that caught the light.

The food arrived hot.

Flatbread blistered from the pan.

A small bowl of vegetables spiced with cumin, turmeric, and chili.

Chai poured into glasses so hot she had to hold hers by the rim.

Elara tore a piece of bread and dipped it into the vegetables. The first bite was sharp with spice, then warm, then sweet beneath the heat.

She closed her eyes briefly.

Ravi laughed softly.

"You will miss the food."

She opened her eyes.

"I already do."

They ate quietly for a few minutes.

A dog slept in the shade near the back of the stall. A child watched them from behind a doorway, then disappeared when Elara smiled.

A truck passed on the road, trailing dust that moved across the scene like a curtain.

When it cleared, the world looked the same.

But she did not.

Ravi wiped his hands on a cloth and leaned back.

"You will write good story?"

"I hope so."

He looked at her.

"Only hope?"

She considered the question.

"I wrote the story I could carry."

Ravi studied her for a moment.

Then nodded once.

"That is good."

She felt unexpected relief.

"Do you think it was wrong not to tell everything?"

Ravi looked toward the road.

"There is no everything."

The answer surprised her.

He continued.

"Even if you write all you saw, it is not everything. Even if you write all you heard, it is not everything. A place is not finished because a visitor understands one part."

Elara let the words move through her.

A place is not finished because a visitor understands one part.

She wished she had written that down.

Maybe she would later.

"You sound like a philosopher," she said.

"No," he replied. "Just a driver."

She smiled.

The world softened for a moment.

Then Ravi added, "But drivers hear many unfinished stories."

Elara looked at him.

"Do they ever finish?"

"Some do. Most change shape."

She thought of the sari in her bag.

Of Arjun somewhere beyond the roads she could see.

Of Luca back in New York, already less powerful in memory than he had been weeks before.

Maybe that was all finishing was.

A story changing shape until it no longer held you the same way.

They drove on.

The landscape slowly changed as the day stretched forward. Desert opened into villages. Villages into busier roads. The air grew thicker again, more populated with scent and sound. The farther they traveled from Pushkar, the more the world seemed to gather itself into density.

Elara watched through the window as women in bright saris moved across fields, their color startling against the earth. Men sat beneath trees, speaking in clusters. Children balanced on bicycles too large for them. Goats wandered where they pleased, indifferent to everything.

She reached for the camera once, then stopped.

Instead, she picked up her notebook.

The pages were filled now.

Fragments.

Lines.

Questions.

Names.

The record of a woman changing in real time.

She turned to a blank page and wrote:

Leaving is not always escape. Sometimes it is the first honest thing you do.

She looked at the words.

Then added:

I came here because I thought distance would free me from what I wanted. Instead, distance showed me how much of wanting was habit.

She paused.

The car moved steadily beneath her.

Then she wrote:

Luca was the pattern. Arjun was the mirror. The desert was the truth.

She stared at the sentence for a long time.

Then closed the notebook.

They reached Delhi after dark.

The city announced itself before it appeared fully.

Traffic first.

Then horns.

Then smoke.

Then light.

So much light.

After the open desert, New Delhi felt almost impossible. Too many cars. Too many voices. Too much movement pressed into too little space. The air was heavier here, layered again with exhaust, street food, incense, damp stone, and the faint sweetness of flowers sold in roadside strands.

Diwali had passed, but traces remained.

Burn marks on the road.

Paper fragments from fireworks gathered along curbs.

Lamps still glowing in windows.

The city had survived its own celebration and continued on.

As cities do.

The hotel gates opened.

The car entered.

Noise softened behind them.

Ravi stopped near the entrance, and for a moment neither of them moved.

The journey was over.

That felt too simple.

Elara gathered her things slowly.

Ravi stepped out and retrieved her bag from the trunk.

When she met him at the curb, he handed it to her carefully.

"Miss Quinn," he said.

She smiled softly.

"Elara."

He looked at her, surprised.

Then nodded.

"Elara."

The name in his voice felt like a small farewell blessing.

"Thank you, Ravi."

"For driving?"

"For more than that."

He inclined his head.

"You were difficult passenger."

She laughed.

A real laugh.

Small, but real.

"I know."

"But good heart," he added.

Her throat tightened.

"I hope so."

"No," he said. "You do."

The certainty in his voice undid her more than she expected.

She reached for his hand. He seemed surprised, but allowed it. She held it briefly in both of hers.

"Please be safe," she said.

He nodded.

"You also."

He stepped back.

She picked up her bag and walked toward the hotel entrance.

At the door, she turned once.

Ravi was still there.

He lifted a hand.

She lifted hers in return.

Then the doors opened, cool air rushed toward her, and the city swallowed the moment.

The hotel room in Delhi was too clean.

Too sealed.

Too quiet in the wrong way.

Elara set her bag on the floor and stood in the center of the room, unsure what to do with herself. The bed was perfectly made. The lamps matched. The bathroom smelled faintly of citrus and polished stone.

Nothing smelled like smoke.

Nothing tasted of dust.

Nothing moved unless she touched it.

She should have been relieved.

Instead, she felt suspended again.

As she had on the flight over.

Between worlds.

She opened her suitcase.

The sari was on top.

She had not remembered placing it there.

But there it was.

Red and gold.

Impossible to ignore.

She lifted it carefully and carried it to the bed, unfolding just enough to see the border catch the lamplight. In the hotel room, away from the desert, it looked even more vivid.

Almost too vivid.

A piece of one world laid across another.

She sat beside it.

For a long time, she only looked.

Then she touched the gold thread with her fingertips.

He had chosen this.

Or sent it.

Or arranged it.

She still did not know which.

The not knowing had become part of the gift.

She would never know everything.

That was the point.

Elara folded the sari again with deliberate care.

This time, she placed it in the carry-on bag she would keep with her.

Not checked.

Not out of reach.

Carried close.

Then she took a shower.

Hot water poured endlessly from the hotel fixture, immediate and abundant. She stood beneath it and thought of the brass vessels at the tent door, of water carried by hand across sand.

Luxury, she realized, was not always abundance.

Sometimes it was effort.

Sometimes it was being cared for in a place where nothing came easily.

The water ran over her hair, down her back, along her arms. Dust disappeared into the drain.

She watched it go.

This time, she did not wish it would stay.

Later, wrapped in a white hotel robe, she sat by the window and looked out over Delhi.

The city moved below, restless and bright. Headlights threaded through roads. Motorbikes slipped between cars. Somewhere, faintly, fireworks still cracked in the distance, leftover celebrations refusing to end cleanly.

Her phone buzzed.

A message from her editor.

These are stunning. Truly. The story has such restraint and atmosphere. Let's talk when you're back. This may be one of your best.

Elara read it twice.

Restraint.

Atmosphere.

She leaned back against the chair and closed her eyes.

The word restraint stayed with her.

Her editor meant craft.

Elara knew it was more than that.

It was the story.

The photographs.

The man.

The line.

The distance.

All of it.

Her phone buzzed again.

A different message.

Unknown number.

For one wild second, her heart stopped.

But it was only the airline confirming her flight.

She let out a breath she had not realized she was holding.

Then laughed softly at herself.

Not cruelly.

Tenderly.

She was still learning.

That was allowed.

The next morning, Ravi was not her driver.

A hotel car took her to the airport.

This should not have mattered.

It did.

The new driver was polite and efficient. He asked if she wanted air conditioning stronger. He asked which terminal. He did not ask what she had seen, or what she had carried, or whether she was quiet because she was tired or because something in her had changed.

Elara watched Delhi pass by the window.

The city at morning was both softer and more ruthless. Vendors opening. Children in uniforms walking to school. Men brushing teeth at roadside taps. Women sweeping dust from thresholds, only for more dust to settle moments later.

Life continuing.

Always.

At the airport, she checked in, passed through security, and found her gate.

The waiting area was full of travelers suspended between places. Families with too many bags. Businessmen speaking into phones. Children sleeping across chairs. Women adjusting scarves. Men reading newspapers.

Elara sat near the window.

Planes moved outside, huge and ordinary.

She placed her carry-on beneath the seat in front of her and rested one hand on it.

The sari was inside.

Her notebook too.

Her camera.

What she had chosen to carry.

Boarding began.

She stood when her group was called.

At the end of the jet bridge, just before stepping onto the plane, she paused.

Not long.

Just enough.

She turned her head slightly, though there was nothing behind her but glass, metal, movement, and strangers.

No desert.

No fair.

No Arjun.

Still, she felt the distance.

Alive.

Uncrossed.

Present.

Then she stepped onto the plane.

The flight lifted out of Delhi into pale morning haze.

Elara watched the city fall away beneath her, the buildings shrinking, the roads becoming lines, the smoke softening everything into memory.

The plane banked.

For one brief moment, beyond the edge of the wing, she thought she saw the land open westward.

Not the desert exactly.

Only the direction of it.

That was enough.

She leaned back in her seat.

Closed her eyes.

And did not try to hold on harder.

That was the difference now.

She had spent so much of her life confusing holding on with love.

But some things were not meant to be held.

Some people were not meant to be followed.

Some distances were not meant to be crossed.

They were meant to be felt.

To change the shape of what you carried home.

Elara opened her eyes as the plane rose higher.

The world below disappeared into cloud.

For the first time since she had arrived in India, she did not wonder what would happen if she had chosen differently.

She had chosen.

That was enough.

And somewhere beneath the cloud, beneath the dust, beneath the vast and unknowable stretch of desert, a man named Arjun Rathore belonged to a world she could not enter.

She let that be true.

She let it hurt.

She let it remain.

Then she turned toward the window, watching light gather along the wing as the plane carried her toward home.

CHAPTER TWENTY-NINE

What Remains

It was winter when she unfolded the sari again.

Not the kind of winter the desert knew.

This was a different cold. Clean. Sharp. Quiet in a way that felt almost reverent. Snow had fallen overnight, settling across the ground in soft, unbroken layers, turning everything outside her window into something hushed and suspended.

Elara stood barefoot on the hardwood floor, a mug of coffee cooling in her hand, watching the morning light move slowly across the white landscape.

Years had passed.

Not in a way she could measure easily.

Not by numbers.

By change.

Her life had filled in.

Not dramatically.

Not all at once.

But steadily.

The apartment in New York had become something else, then something else again. Cities had come and gone. Work had deepened. Her photography had changed. Her eye had changed with it. She still traveled, still told stories, still followed light across the world.

But she no longer chased it.

That was the difference.

The men had changed too.

Or maybe she had.

There had been others after India.

Of course there had.

She had fallen in love again.

Or something close to it.

More than once.

But not the way she used to.

Not with the same hunger that mistook intensity for truth.

Not with the same quiet belief that if she just stayed long enough, loved hard enough, endured enough, something unstable would become steady.

She had learned.

Not all at once.

Not cleanly.

But undeniably.

And still—

Some things remained.

She set the coffee down on the counter and crossed the room slowly, her fingers brushing along the edge of a wooden table worn smooth by time. The house was quiet. Not empty.

Quiet.

A chosen quiet.

In the corner of the living room stood a large box.

It had been there for years.

Moved from place to place.

Never unpacked fully.

Never forgotten.

Elara knelt beside it.

For a moment, she didn't open it.

She rested her hand on the lid.

As if the act of touching it alone was enough to bring everything back.

Then she lifted it.

Inside, beneath layers of folded paper, old photographs, and journals she no longer needed but could not discard, lay the fabric.

Red.

Gold.

Unchanged.

The sari had not faded.

Not really.

The color still held something alive inside it, something that refused to dull with time. The gold thread still caught the light, even here, even now, even so far from the desert that had once given it meaning.

Elara lifted it slowly.

The weight was the same.

That surprised her.

She had expected it to feel lighter.

Or heavier.

Instead, it felt exactly as it had.

Present.

She carried it across the room and laid it gently on the floor beneath the Christmas tree.

The tree stood tall and green, lit softly with white lights that reflected in the windows and the glass ornaments that hung from its branches. Outside, snow continued to fall in slow, quiet patterns.

The red and gold fabric spread beneath it like a memory made visible.

For years, she had questioned this.

The first time she placed it there, it had felt wrong.

Too intimate.

Too personal.

Too connected to a version of herself she had not yet understood.

Now—

It felt like something else.

Not shame.

Not nostalgia.

Not longing.

Recognition.

Elara sat back on her heels and looked at it.

Really looked.

She did not see him the way she once had.

Not first.

She saw herself.

A younger woman.

Standing at the edge of something she did not yet understand.

Drawn to heat.

To danger.

To the illusion that proximity meant belonging.

She saw the pattern.

Luca.

Before him, others.

Men who burned fast and bright and left her standing in the aftermath, wondering why wanting had not been enough.

She saw it clearly now.

Without judgment.

Without the sharp edge of regret.

Just truth.

And then—

She saw him.

Arjun.

Not as a man she had lost.

But as a man she had never been meant to have.

The distinction mattered.

It changed everything.

He had not been hers to keep.

He had not been hers to save.

He had not been hers to follow.

He had been—

A moment.

A mirror.

A line she did not cross.

And that had changed her more than crossing it ever would have.

Elara leaned forward slightly, her fingers brushing the gold thread along the edge of the sari.

She closed her eyes.

And for a moment—

She was back there.

The desert air warm against her skin.

The smell of cumin and dust and smoke.

The sound of camels shifting in the night.

The weight of silence between words.

His voice.

Low.

Steady.

Careful.

You cannot come back from every line you cross.

Her breath caught.

Even now.

Even years later.

But she hadn't crossed it.

That was the truth that had taken her the longest to understand.

Not crossing the line had not been a loss.

It had been the first time she chose herself over the story she wanted to believe.

She opened her eyes.

The room returned.

The tree.

The snow.

The life she had built.

And then—

Another memory surfaced.

Not from the desert.

From later.

From a different time.

A different man.

DV Sharma.

She hadn't said his name out loud in years.

Not because she had forgotten.

Because she hadn't needed to.

He had loved her.

Fully.

Openly.

Without restraint.

And she had known.

Even then.

Even as she smiled.

Even as she accepted the gifts.

Even as she let him believe in something she could never give back.

She had known.

The red and gold sari.

Her breath caught slightly as the memory sharpened.

The way he had carried it.

Carefully.

Proudly.

As if offering her something sacred.

As if placing something in her hands that meant more than she could understand at the time.

And she had taken it.

That was the part that stayed with her.

Not that he loved her.

But that she had taken something she knew she would never honor in the way it deserved.

For years, she had felt shame in that.

Sharp.

Persistent.

But now—

Now she understood something she hadn't then.

She had been a different woman.

Not cruel.

Not careless.

Unaware.

And awareness changes everything.

Elara pulled the edge of the sari slightly, adjusting it beneath the tree.

Her movements were gentle.

Intentional.

"I'm sorry," she whispered.

Not to Arjun.

To the man who had loved her when she didn't yet know how to receive love without turning it into something else.

The apology did not feel heavy.

It felt complete.

She sat back and drew her knees up slightly, wrapping her arms loosely around them.

The lights on the tree flickered softly, reflecting in the gold thread.

For a long time, she sat there.

Not thinking.

Not analyzing.

Just… being.

And then, quietly, the understanding came.

Not all love is meant to be lived.

Some love is meant to show you who you are.

Who you've been.

Who you are becoming.

She had been the woman who chased.The woman who stayed too long.

The woman who mistook fire for warmth.

She was no longer that woman.

And she was no longer the woman who took love she could not return without understanding its cost.

She had become something else.

A woman who could feel deeply…

without losing herself in it.

A woman who could walk away…

without calling it failure.

A woman who could hold memory…

without needing to rewrite it into something it was not.

Elara stood slowly.

The room felt warm now.

Grounded.

Complete.

She walked to the window and looked out at the snow-covered world beyond.

It was quiet.

Still.

Whole in its own way.

Behind her, the red and gold sari lay beneath the tree, no longer a symbol of confusion or regret.

A marker.

Of everything she had lived.

Everything she had learned.

Everything she had chosen not to become.

And everything she had finally allowed herself to be.

She placed her hand lightly against the glass.

Cold met warmth.

Somewhere in the world, beyond cities and time and the life she now lived, a man named Arjun Rathore still walked within a desert that had shaped him long before she arrived.

She did not wonder if he thought of her.

That was no longer the question.

The question had always been—

What did she carry forward?

And now she knew.

Not him.

Not the story.

Not the fire.

The choice.

Always the choice.

Elara closed her eyes for a moment.

Then opened them.

And stepped fully into the life that was hers.

EPILOGUE

Months later, she returned.

The crowds were gone. And with them, the reason most people came.

What remained was something else entirely. Something quieter. Something she had not finished with.

Where there had once been a city of canvas and color, there was now only open desert.

The sand had smoothed itself over the footprints. The air held no trace of smoke, or spice, or song. Only wind.

And silence.

Elara stood at the edge of it, her boots sinking slightly into the soft earth, her scarf lifting behind her in the breeze.

New York had come back to her quickly. The noise. The rhythm. The expectations. Meetings stacked on meetings. Conversations that skimmed the surface of things.

She had moved through it all exactly as she had before.

And yet, nothing felt the same.

It was not that something was missing. It was that something had been added.

Something she could not name. Could not explain. Would not dare try to reduce to language.

So she came back.

Not for answers.

For recognition.

She closed her eyes and could still feel it — the pulse of drums in her chest, the low murmur of voices in languages she did not speak but somehow understood, the weight of something ancient pressing just beneath the surface of everything.

And him.

That was the part she could not explain. Would never try to.

Arjun had not asked her to stay.

He had not followed her when she left.

There had been no declarations. No promises stretched thin across impossible distance.

Only a look.

One that held centuries. One that said everything words would have diminished.

She had carried it with her ever since.

Not like a memory.

Like a knowing.

A small group of Raika men moved in the distance, guiding the last of the camels across the horizon. Their silhouettes blurred against the rising heat, steady and timeless.

Life continued, as it always had.

As it always would.

Elara reached into her bag and pulled out the photograph.

She had not remembered taking it.

Not consciously.

But there it was.

A frame of golden light and dust, a blur of motion, and in the center, unmistakable.

Him.

Not looking at the camera. Not even aware of it.

Looking at her.

She traced the edge of the image with her thumb, her breath catching just slightly — not in pain, but in recognition.

Some connections did not ask to be defined. They simply existed.

Outside of logic. Outside of time.

A gust of wind swept across the desert, lifting the sand in a soft spiral around her feet.

For a moment, she thought she heard it again — the faint echo of bells, of voices, of something just beyond reach.

She did not turn.

She did not chase it.

She smiled.

And stepped forward.

Not away from it.

But carrying it with her.

ACKNOWLEDGMENTS

In 1997, Gordy and Karen took my mom and me on a journey across India, one we experienced together, every step of the way.

It was on that trip that I first stepped into Pushkar, into its color and energy and something I couldn't quite name, but never forgot.

To my mom, thank you for sharing that experience with me.

And to Gordy and Karen, thank you for your extraordinary generosity, and for a journey that stayed long after we returned.

This story begins there.

ABOUT THE AUTHOR

Christine Zanjanipour is a writer, entrepreneur, and storyteller drawn to the spaces where experience and emotion intersect. Her work often explores themes of connection, memory, and the moments that quietly shape who we become.

Inspired in part by a formative journey through India, The Desert Between Us reflects her love of atmospheric storytelling and the idea that not all encounters can be easily explained.

Christine lives in Colorado, where she continues to write and build a body of work centered on meaningful experiences and intentional living.

Before I Had The Words

❧

"Some places do not simply become memories.
They become part of who you are.

These photographs were taken during a journey through India in 1997, including time spent at the Pushkar Camel Fair in Rajasthan.

Long before this book existed, that journey quietly planted something within me:
a deeper awareness of presence, perspective, simplicity, and gratitude.

Even now, decades later, those moments still remind me how much beauty exists in the world when we slow down enough to truly see it."

EXOTIC RESORTS &
ADVENTURES
PUSHKAR FAIR 1997

Dear Friends,

Welcome to the Pushkar Fair 97

PUSHKAR : The Spiritual Paradise

This temple town, situated 13 kms. north-west of Ajmer at the base of 'Nag Pahar' (or snake mountain) which forms a part of the chain of the Aravali range, stands as a testimony to the rich cultural and religious heritage of India. The town itself is picturesquely situated on the lake with hills on three sides and on the fourth side, the sands drifted from the plains of Marwar have formed a complete bar to the waters of the lake, which has no outlet, though the filteration through the sand hills is considerable.

"Pushkar is the most sacred place of the Hindus in India. It is the " King of sacred places," just as Benaras is their 'guru' of preceptor. No pilgrimage to Badri Narain (Himalyas) Jagannath (Orissa) Rameshwaram (Tamil Nadu), Dwarka (Gujarat) the four principal Hindu places of pilgrimage, is complete till the pilgrims bath in the sacred waters of Pushkar.

The holy town was equally sacred to Buddhists as is evident from the four stone inscriptions of the second century B.C. in the Buddhist 'stupa' at Sanchi in Bhopal (M.P.).

This beautiful lake surrounded by bathing ghats has its religious significance rooted in a myth according to the Padam Puran, Lord Brahma the creatór of the Univers, was in search of a suitable place to perform a yagna (ritual associated with sacred fire) while contemplating, a lotus fell from his hand on the earth and water spurled from three places. Brahma descended the earth and named the place Pushkar, after the lotus. One of them was Pushkar and Brahma decided to perform his yagna here.

Temple and Ghats in Pushkar.

As the fame of Pushkar spread to different and far flung corners at the country, many princely houses, and business houses constructed temples, houses and gardens in Pushkar and it thus prospered.

Important and Historical Temples Varahji Temple

The temple of Varahji was built by the Chauhan King Arnoraja (1123-1150 A.D.) who also got the Pushkar lake repaired.

(ii) Temple of Brahmaji is situated towards the farther end of the lake. It is reputed to be the only temple in the country dedicated to Brahmaji. The image of Brahmaji has four faces and is in a sitting posture.

(iii) Sri Rama Vaikuntha Temple :

This is the most imposing of the modern temple and is situated at the entrance to the town. It belongs to the Sri Vaishnava sect of the Hindus. Which was founded by Shri Ramanuja Charya who flourished in the eleventh century.

The fair is also the biggest camel market beside camels, horses and Bullocks are sold and bought here. The people in their colourful attires enhance the cheerful mood of the fair. Rajasthan Tourism presents cultural programmes during this time, bringing to life an oriental charm and beauty. Pushkar abounds in temple and also has the temple of Lord Brahma (Lord of Creation). This is the only temple dedicated to Brahma.

Ghats : Gau Ghat

This is the largest Ghat in Pushkar. A Janana Ghat for women was built on it in 1913 A.D. by the help of queen Mery of England, Maharana of Udaipur and Maharana of Jodhpur and there are 51 other ghats around the holy lake of Pushkar.

www.ingramcontent.com/pod-product-compliance
Lightning Source LLC
LaVergne TN
LVHW100514110826
845146LV00002B/630

* 9 7 9 8 9 9 3 9 0 1 3 8 1 *